THE ELEMENTALIST

/ / / /

J.R. RAIN
&
MATTHEW S. COX

FOUR ELEMENTS TRILOGY

The Elementalist
The Black Rose
The Wakefield Curse

Published by
Crop Circle Books
212 Third Crater, Moon

Printed in the United States of America.

ISBN-9781091580206

Chapter One
The Dame

I see it again in my dreams.

The fire... blazing across the night sky.

It is the third such time I have seen it, but this time is different. This time, I awaken, gasping, and covered in sweat. I am certain, yes, beyond certain that my hands are glowing.

Dreaming... I'm obviously dreaming.

I lay my head back down on my pillow, tucking my hands under the covers, and fall asleep again, dreaming of rushing water, blowing wind, shaking earth... and a raging fire...

***

The day started like any other day in recent memory. Ordinary.

I'd been sitting in my office eating a cold bologna sandwich, watching highlights from California Tech's worst season in twenty years when *she* walked into my life.

She was a dead ringer for Veronica Lake: pale skin, silky hair swept over one eye, and bow-shaped lips plumped up to a quarter-pout. The girl had curves in all the right places and moved with fluid ease, more floated than walked. Chic high heels supported a pair of shapely legs peeking from beneath a mid-thigh navy skirt and matching blazer. For a millisecond, I caught a glimpse of lacy white camisole as she peered at me through my half-open office door.

I blinked and turned off the YouTube video. In fact, I almost pinched my arm.

Before I made too much a fool of myself, I swallowed the giant mouthful of sandwich as discreetly and fast as possible, cringing at the bite of strong mustard.

She stood there like a shy, demure creature not quite sure if she would be safe stepping into my domain. The look suited her, though—and I couldn't quite say why—it didn't make her come off as a helpless damsel, more like she deliberately put on an air of harmlessness. An act, perhaps. My instincts said to be careful with this one, that I stared into the pretty blue eyes of a trap.

Beautiful women didn't exactly grace my humble office often. Hell, lately, clients in general rarely graced my office. These days, investigation gigs were few and far between, which I didn't mind much. My landlord, however, did mind. Especially when the lack of clients caused my rent payment to wind up being late. Unfortunately, I wasn't quite pretty enough to bat my eyelashes and pay with my good looks, so I actually had to work a case every now and then.

"Come on in," I said, before taking a sip from my lukewarm can of Diet Coke.

The woman had been crying, that much was obvious. I didn't consider myself an ace detective for nothing. She crept in the office door, looking a little bit hesitant and a lot beautiful. Her misty blue eyes warned me she had a story that would get me so choked up I wouldn't even care if she could pay me. Yeah, she was *that* gorgeous. *That* classy. And *that* vulnerable. Something about her struck a chord in me. Up until that moment, if anyone had asked me if I believed in love at first sight, I would've laughed at them. But the more I stared into those teary eyes of hers, the more I felt like a high school kid who unexpectedly wound up face to face with his crush, simultaneously thrilled and wanting to run away screaming.

"Can I help you?" I asked, my voice squeakier than I would have liked.

"Are you a real private investigator?" she asked in a shy voice not far above a whisper. I detected a trace of awe in it, too, as if she'd placed private detectives somewhere between Bigfoot and the Second Coming.

"I am. To the envy of all my friends," I said, milking it. "Please, sit. I have coffee if you'd like some... I have tea, too. I think."

She thought about it longer than I would have liked. These days, people's need for private eyes has diminished thanks to the internet. Computers and broadband had pushed a lot of us out of work. Most people could track—aka stalk—anyone they wanted online. Although I didn't consider myself a professional stalker, I had once made a good living by locating people who didn't want to be found. These days, I mostly dealt with cases from the odd housewife who suspected her husband of cheating or the even rarer husband who suspected his wife of cheating. Every so often, I had someone asking me to background check someone—usually owners of small business around here. And twice, I tracked down guys not paying child support. I tried to avoid taking missing persons cases around here, since nine times out of ten, they either went nowhere or ended up as a body in the woods.

I got why people thought private dicks were sleazy. I *felt* sleazy following sleazy people doing sleazy things. I felt especially dirty after I took zoom-lens evidence photos of marital cheating in progress. However, I took whatever work came my way. It was a seedy job, but somebody had to do it.

At first, I expected this girl to say her hubby cheated on her and she needed me to find proof. If she had a husband, they couldn't have been married for long. I figured her for maybe twenty-one or so.

She looked way too... *nice* to have sex outside of marriage. Yeah, a real angel face. My second thought was that she should definitely get back at the jerk—with me, of course.

Okay, maybe I *was* one of those sleazy detectives.

Eventually, she nodded and came in. "Yes, coffee would be fine."

I rushed out of my chair, banging my knee in the process, and limped around my crumb-strewn desk. "Cream and sugar?" I only had dehydrated Coffee-Mate, but 'cream' sounded classier.

"Yes, and yes," she said, which I thought sounded adorable.

My hand shook a little as I reached for the guest mug. I poured her a cup of my best java, which is the only kind of java I drank. I might skimp on the office rent, but never the coffee. *Never.*

"Is now a good time to talk?" she asked. "Or should I make an appointment?"

"You're in luck," I said. I hadn't had anyone call me for an appointment in maybe two months. "My next appointment just canceled. I'm all yours."

Boy, sounding sleazier and sleazier.

"Really?" she said, her eyes innocent and trusting.

Okay, now I felt like shit for lying to her. I sighed, then brought the coffee over and handed it to her. She looked up at me with what I would classify as gratitude, so I coughed up the truth. "No. I'm just making a joke. I didn't have any other client. *Lying* is what private eyes do sometimes to get information. We're good at lying. I'm good at it."

"That's not really something to be proud of," she said, avoiding eye contact. "Lying, I mean. Lies can cause a lot of damage."

"You're right, sorry. But you might think differently if my, um, skills were able to help you." I slipped back around my desk with my coffee mug in hand. "Speaking of which, how can I help you?"

She processed what I'd said and nearly got up to leave. I mean, I'm not a mind reader or anything, but I saw her questioning... everything. Luckily, my coffee must have been that good—or the warm mug felt comforting in her hand. Or maybe my encouraging smile did her in… or the relaxing ambiance of my simple office with its cluttered desk and foldout client chairs. At least she wasn't put off by the scar on the right side of my neck…a nasty sucker that reached up almost to my ear and plummeted to well below my collar bone.

Or, perhaps, she was that desperate.

"I need help, Mister...."

"Long," I said. "Max Long."

She nodded. "I need help, Mr. Long."

I nodded along with her. "What kind of help?"

She sipped from her coffee mug, her pinkie finger sticking out at a 90-degree angle. She'd had etiquette training, which didn't surprise me. This town had old money, and a lot of people who still held onto past niceties. Nine families had most of the wealth in the area, and they'd had it for a couple centuries at least. People around here referred to them as the Founding Families, since they'd initially settled the area. Etiquette training still remained popular for the upper class, like they clung to the old 'royals and peasants' mentality. This girl obviously had taken the white gloves and ankles-kept-crossed seminars. She exuded upper class—except for the haughtiness.

"Someone killed my sister and her husband."

I was about to lift my coffee mug when I paused. Steam wafted up between us, drifting past the face of the blonde woman in front of me. I'd heard about the deaths, of course. "That was your sister? The animal attack in the woods?"

She nodded and looked down, fighting tears. Eventually, she collected herself and sighed. "You would think the woods here crawled with bears and wolves, based on all the animal attacks."

"You disagree with the official findings?"

"Damn straight I disagree."

"I'm sorry for your loss, but what exactly are you looking for me to do?"

"I know it wasn't an animal attack, Mr. Long. I want to hire you to find proof of that. I want you to prove that something else is going on in these damn woods. Once and for all, I want you to help this town find answers for why so many people here die horrific deaths or just disappear."

I blinked, absorbing her words. I hadn't worked a wrongful death case in a long time. My cases tended to be lightweights. Heck, my last job had been undercover work at the Shadow Pines Hospital, trying to find out who'd been stealing from their blood supply. I never did find the bastard, although I was pretty sure the hospital was haunted as all get out. Moving shadows, disembodied footsteps and breathing sounds, and the overall disconcerting feeling that someone was watching me. Afterward, I had dreams of that place, nightmares where a tall man with a long face and Hollywood hair told me to forget what I saw. Of course, I could never quite remember what I had supposedly seen, but the dreams were weird as hell.

She bit her lip. "Sheriff Waters and her team of klutzes aren't saying much. It makes me wonder whose side they're on. It's why I came to you."

I nodded. "What's your name?"

"Crystal Bradbury."

Aww damn. There it was. Bradbury… one of the Founding Families. I said the dumbest thing possible after hearing that. "You live in town?"

She shook her head. "Ironside."

Okay, that surprised me. If someone with that name didn't live *in* town, it meant something. It might mean she just happened to have a surname that matched one of the oldest, most influential families in the area, but I doubted that. Shadow Pines' former mayor, Sterling Bradbury, had a reputation for being a real piece of work—that's polite speak for asshole. Fortunately, he'd been eaten by a bear or something out in the woods…

like so many other people in this place. It's an absolute wonder why anyone still went out into the forest for recreation. With all the animal attacks around here, you'd think everyone would be hiding in their houses with the windows boarded up.

Another thing stood out to me. This girl didn't resemble Sterling in the slightest. Though, sometimes genetics did weird things. I knew the nearby town of Ironside, of course. Locals called it a poor man's Shadow Pines. At least, that's what my generation always called it back in high school. Troublemakers often ended up being sent there to finish high school with the 'less desirables.' The town had a fair number of steel mills and mines, all started by the Founding Families years ago. Only a handful continued to operate these days.

Ironside also had some factories and a lot of nature tourism. With mountains on one side, forest everywhere else, it had become a beacon for people rebelling against urbanization. Some called it a sister city. I always thought of it as an annoying little brother city. Then again, I was biased. I grew up in Shadow Pines, and good or bad—mind you, this place had a lot of bad—I loved my creepy little hometown.

She must have seen the surprised look on my face, because she added, "You could say I started in Shadow Pines, and finished in Ironside."

I put two and two together and figured she'd done something bad. Or at least socially horrible. Bad enough to be cast out, most likely. Or at least kept at arms' length to protect the rest of the family's reputation. I'd probably have known exactly what she'd done if I bothered paying attention to the upper class around here, but I never understood the fascination with that. Why would working-class people care who a celebrity dated, or freak out if they got in trouble with the law? I would never understand that the same way I couldn't fathom how people in the UK fawned all over their royals.

"You were a problem child," I said.

She gave me a half smile. I had the feeling she liked to have fun, to enjoy life, but recent events had dragged her down. A murdered sister would do that to you.

"I was just being me," she said, "but the Bradburys had a name to uphold."

"Your father used to be the Mayor?"

"Yup. Mayor, asshole, you pick," she said.

I recalled seeing him years ago. He'd smacked one of his sons, Arthur I think, over at the Pines Café. The boy had to be twelve or so at the time and a paparazzi caught the moment of the slap with near perfect timing. That photo was everywhere for months. Some called it the 'slap heard 'round the world.'

"We shouldn't speak ill of the dead."

"And why's that?"

"Because they can't defend themselves."

"Are you sure about that?" she asked cryptically.

"Umm..."

"Anyway, I told Dana not to go out there. I mean, who wanders off for a party deep in the woods around Shadow Pines these days? How many people have to die before people get the idea that it's not safe here? If you ask me, it was a godsend that I was sent out of this town, even if the boarding high school had been more like a prison."

"That bad?"

"Compared to what I'd been used to, it felt like prison. Ironside has been good to me. It's kept me alive."

She had a point. The sheer number of deaths in this town has been staggering, along with numerous supposed incidents of supernatural activity. Spontaneous combustion. Reports of hauntings. UFOs sightings up the wazoo. Of wolves running free in the streets.

And, of course, the daddy of all rumors...

Vampires.

Yup, vampires. As in bloodsucking fiends. Guess where my mind went while investigating the guy stealing blood from the hospital? Yeah... a rational person would've assumed some wacko with a vampire complex. Me? For some reason, as much as I couldn't believe it, I half expected it to be a real vampire. Probably because the basement hallway, according to witnesses, always stank of rotting bodies whenever blood went missing. This town had a history of such crazy stories, and, with all the disappearances, I couldn't help but wonder if the rumors might be more than a bunch of scared (and bored) locals running their mouths. Hell, the newspaper got a hold of the blood theft story and went crazy with it. People had been petitioning the mayor for years to make vampires illegal. You can't make this stuff up!

Anyway, all were whisperings, of course. All were laughed off. Nervously, that is. Truth was, something was happening in this town, something damn strange. A lot went on just below the ability of most people to realize it. One would think that with all of the strange occurrences, I would actually be a *busy* private eye, but that wasn't the case. Most people didn't talk about the strange happenings, and fewer still hired me to look into them. Most people swept them under the proverbial rug. Most residents, in my view, were hiding a lot of secrets.

A helluva lot of secrets.

Then again, I could be wrong, too.

Over the years and decades, Crystal's family had suffered some of the greatest losses. And the tragedy evidently continues...

I recalled the case since I'd seen a bit of it on the news, but not the details. A young-ish married couple slipped away from a party for a quiet walk in the woods and never returned. The authorities called it another random animal attack in the woods. One of dozens over the years. At the time, the names had been withheld. Truth was, I had forgotten about them until now.

"The police claimed a mountain lion attacked

them," I said. "What makes you suspect something else?"

"Because she called me and told me something was following them."

A cold chill swept over me. "Something or someone?"

"She said something."

"Did she happen to say *what* followed them?"

"No. She was too busy screaming."

"You heard your sister die? Over the phone?"

"Every strangled gasp and shriek, Mr. Long. Now, do you see why I want answers?"

"Yeah…" I picked up my notepad and asked the usual array of questions to establish the where and when.

Crystal hadn't heard a big cat in the background. No growling, roaring, nothing. Nor did her sister mention a cat.

"Felines are rather stealthy. Perhaps she'd been ambushed?" I asked. "Sorry if I sound a bit oafish and insensitive, but there's no way of tiptoeing around some of this stuff. I don't mean to be cruel, just trying to take the most direct path to the answer."

"I understand. It's all right. And no, I don't think she was ambushed. Dana wouldn't have had the time to call me if a big cat pounced on her without warning. She called me while running away from something. She said *it's* following us. I heard them running, then some grunts… and... all the screaming —" She broke down crying.

I sat there offering a comforting gaze, patiently waiting for her to regain her composure, wondering if I should comfort her, but concluding that would be overstepping my position. Dammit.

"She begged for her life, Mr. Long. Begged."

"People don't usually plead with animals not to kill them."

"Now you know why I came to you. The police are no help. They decided it was an animal before they even went to the place it happened. As far as they're concerned, a mountain lion did it and there's no point arguing the point with them."

"Yeah, I can see that."

I was with Crystal. Something didn't seem right, and I was happy to take the case.

More than happy.

My landlord would be too.

Chapter Two
Pins and Needles

The Shadow Pines Sheriff's Office was always surprisingly busy for a small town. Today was no exception.

I parked in one of the spaces lining the edges of the town square. The city hall occupied the center of the west side, the police station on the north face, both nestled among an array of fancy boutiques, little bistros, and overpriced gift shops. Women in sneakers power-walked during their lunch breaks, young mothers with strollers meandered along while texting, and a frazzled hot dog vendor struggled to keep up with a long line. Maintenance workers swept up popcorn from last night's latest Movie in the Square showing of *The Wizard of Oz*. I hadn't gone. It seemed more of a date-night thing. I didn't have a date with anything other than a bottle of cheap bourbon. Yeah, that's how low I'd sunk since my last girlfriend left me.

Smart girl.

After locking my gun in the glove box, I hopped out of my pickup and walked past a stream of deputies emerging from the entrance of the sheriff's office, located under the clock tower, determination in their strides as if on high alert. Another rash of killings tended to put the law on edge. Years ago, I'd worked with Sheriff Justine Waters on a missing person case, and that person had stayed missing, sadly. Private eyes and cops alike had that tragedy in common. Sometimes, our cases *didn't* get solved. Indeed, the cops had their cold cases, and I had mine.

Anyway, I flashed my ID at the check-in window and the desk sergeant buzzed me in. I made my way through crowded halls that reminded me more of a precinct in New York than a small town in the mountains, and found Sheriff Waters sitting at her expansive desk, surrounded by far too much paperwork. I rapped on the open door and stuck my head in. "Have a minute, Sheriff?"

Her hard green eyes widened in an expression approaching surprise. "Max... You have that look about you that suggests you're working an actual case."

"Stranger things have happened. Can we talk?"

"Have a seat."

I entered and sat across from her. With her mouse-brown hair glowing radiantly in the slanting sunlight, she might have looked beautiful. Problem was, we had dated not too long ago, and some of that shine had worn off. We worked much better as friends, it turned out. No, scratch that—we worked better as colleagues. 'Friends' was pushing it. The break up hadn't been smooth, to say the least. Turned out, I tended to become a bit mean when I felt rejected.

"You're here about the Dana Bradbury case," she said. "Unless you want to apologize."

"For what?"

"For being an ass."

"I was lashing out."

"I didn't deserve to be called all those... names."

Truth be told, I couldn't remember what I'd called her, so upset had I been at being dumped. I might have mentioned something about being both uptight and loose with her morals.

"No, you didn't."

"Well?"

"Well, what?"

"My apology?"

"That was months ago..."

"Being called a slut with a stick up her ass doesn't just go away."

I sighed. Why did she care so much about an apology? I didn't know, but I needed her help, and her being mad at me did no good. "Fine, I'm sorry for being an ass."

"Say it like you mean it."

"Have you always been this controlling?"

"I have. You were just too smitten to notice."

I chuckled at that. "Fine. I'm sorry like I meant it."

"You're not supposed to say that last part. You're supposed to... emote it."

"Lordy. Can we get back to the case?"

"Sure, but can you quit looking at me like that."

"Like what?" I ask.

"Like you're still in love with me."

I snorted, and so did she. We got along fine, even swimmingly. But dating... not so much. We were both sort of pig-headed. Okay, maybe more than 'sort of.' Trouble was, I'd really fallen for her, and I was too prideful to let it show. That's why the breakup had stung.

"How did you know I was here about the killings?" I asked, shaking off the sadness that threatened to overwhelm me... yet again.

Justine shrugged. "The younger sister was in here yesterday, raising hell, not happy with our findings. Wasn't hard to deduce she decided to look elsewhere for help. And last time I checked, you're the only private *dick* working in town."

"The only and best." I noted the emphasis on *dick*... sigh.

"Sad but true. But I'm afraid Crystal's only throwing away her money. We confirmed a big cat was responsible for the attack. Even had a forensic odontologist and a carnivore biologist confirm the wounds were consistent with claw and bite marks from a large feline. Not to mention, we found fur and blood from the animal all over the scene. Oh, lastly, the husband had the animal's blood under his nails."

"He put up a fight."

"Tried to."

"Was the cat found?"

"No. We looked."

"I'm sure you did. Five whole minutes? Since when is the Shadow Pines Sheriff Department big game trackers?"

She laughed. "Such an ass. We teamed up with the local park rangers. No sign of the cat, but they are still on the lookout."

"Should the town be on lockdown? You know, with a big cat on the loose?"

"Refer to my prior comment," she said. "The part about being an ass."

"It's a serious question. Once those suckers get a taste for man, all bets are off."

"We're doing our best to keep the town safe, Max."

I took in some air. "Crystal heard her sister screaming, Sheriff. She didn't hear anything else. No growling or roaring or even meowing. Dana said nothing about a cat, but she did say they were being stalked by something in the woods."

"I know, Max. I spoke with Crystal at length. Dana never mentioned what was stalking her over the phone before she stopped talking... and started, you know..."

"Dying?"

"Yeah, that. Anyway, it could have been a big cat stalking her, and based on the evidence, it was, in fact, a big cat. If not, what else? A bear? If so, then why no evidence of a bear? A man? You really think there is a man out there killing people and making it look like a cat did it?"

"I'm just doing my job, Justine."

"That's Sheriff Justine to you, pal."

I sighed. "Fine. *Sheriff.* Look, my client isn't happy with the findings, and I'm here to see if anything got... um..."

"Missed? Overlooked? Is that what kind of department you think I run, Max?"

"That Private Dick Max to you, missy."

"Oh god, that sounds all kind of wrong."

I laughed. She... almost smiled. Good enough.

"No. I don't think you cut corners or misread the findings, Sheriff. I'm here at the behest of my client, to serve her in whatever capacity I can. I'm being asked to look deeper into the case, and so I am. It's how I make a buck."

"Give her money back, Max. There is no case here."

"One problem," I said. "I already paid my rent with it."

She snorted. "What did I ever see you in you?"

"My prowess in the bedroom?"

"Yeah, maybe. I do miss that. Don't get any funny ideas. I don't sleep around with assholes."

"I'm not an asshole."

"You hurt me. That makes you an asshole."

"I'm sorry."

She drummed her fingers on her oversized desk, looked at me sideways. "What else did you need?"

"The autopsy report?"

"You can read it in here, but it doesn't leave my desk."

"Thank you."

"Wait here."

"On pins and needles."

She laughed once. "Such a dork. Be right back."

I couldn't help but smile as she left.

J.R. RAIN AND MATTHEW S. COX

Chapter Three
Nature

I drove out to Pine Grove, a popular campground located roughly three miles southeast of town.

A large gift shop styled to resemble a log cabin sat beside an expansive dirt parking lot that held an assortment of Range Rovers, Mercedes SUVs, and a couple Saabs. People came here for two primary reasons: hiking out to a spot where they'd camp, or taking the shorter trail to the water and going kayaking. From the number of vehicles here, people hadn't cared much about the recent attack.

Through my preliminary research, I'd discovered that no less than fourteen people in the last ten years had been killed or had gone missing in this area. There should be a big sign above the entrance to the parking lot that read: "Enter at Your Own Risk."

Well, I was entering, and I was risking. I had a job to do, after all.

Besides, I'd been in these woods plenty of times. Dozens, in fact. Hundreds maybe. I had grown up in Shadow Pines. The forest surrounding the town had dozens of hangout spots. These days, they were a favorite venue for teen raves (although back in my day we called it partying), even from kids in surrounding areas, though other than Ironside, the nearest town sat roughly a half hour drive away. Either way, it was a coming-of-age tradition that Shadow Pines kids would go out into the forest and cut loose (read: get high and drunk). Anyway, despite all the deaths, disappearances, and reports of animal attacks, people still partied hard in these woods—and camped in them as well. Shadow Pines residents were either a stubborn bunch, or not the sharpest knives in the drawer. Sometimes, the two went hand in hand.

I got out of my old beat up F150 and shut the door quietly. Hey, no need to alert whatever the hell was out here; after all, *something* killed those campers.

Relax, Max, I thought, reciting my go-to, rhyming mantra.

I surveyed the woods, taking in a deep lungful of fresh air, my .44 revolver tucked in a shoulder holster on my left side. This land was my land, my home. I wasn't going to let anything keep me from enjoying them... and I damn well wasn't going to let anything keep me from doing my job. I shouldered my backpack, walked across the parking area, and started up the winding dirt path.

There it was… The Shadow Pines stubbornness.

Or stupidity.

Anyone growing up here had that stubbornness (and/or stupidity) embedded in their upbringing, almost a God-given right to be slaughtered here in these woods. That, and the back country truly sang a siren call to people in a small town with little options for entertainment. My father always said in places like this, people only had the three Fs to amuse themselves: fighting, food, and… well, guess. Probably why the town had three elementary schools and no university. By the time most of us got out of high school, we realized if we didn't escape soon, we'd be trapped here for the rest of our lives. For anyone but those in the Founding Families, that didn't sound like such a great idea. They had the means to vacation wherever they cared to, buy any expensive toys they wanted. The rest of us, well… we either went shooting in the woods, got into random fights to pass the time, or repopulated the town. Hell, something like thirty percent of the Sheriff's office's time was spent dragging drunken, amorous high schoolers out of the forest.

The morning was unusually cool for late June. I wore a light jacket, jeans, and hiking boots. I'd packed two big bottles of water plus three peanut butter and honey sandwiches. More than enough for a day hike out to the crime scene.

Thanks to my old sweetheart, the sheriff, I knew precisely where the attack had occurred. Truth be told, I had been to the same spot at least two or three times. Hell, almost everyone in Shadow Pines over the age of sixteen had been out there at least once. The site was adjacent to a beautiful waterfall and a clear pool of fresh water. Probably the most photographed area within twenty miles. To think that's where Dana Bradbury and her husband, enjoying a small party with nary a care in the world, would meet their end... Crystal had told me that the husband, Luke, came from LA. Good chance she'd pulled him away from the party to show him the 'most beautiful spot in the USA.'

I shook my head at the tragedy of it all, and put boots to the ground. I had a lot of distance to cover. And, if this had been something more than an animal attack, their decision to walk to the falls hadn't been *that* critical in causing their deaths. Meaning, whoever murdered them would've done it wherever they could. Though, Dana and Luke obligingly going off alone into the trees probably hurried the process along. The more I thought about it as I walked, the more my gut agreed with Crystal about this not being the work of a rogue mountain lion.

The trail continued on through old-growth woods, filled to overflowing with sprawling spruces and giant oaks. An extensive canopy mostly blotted out the sun, dimming the underbrush and offering no shortage of places for feral cats—or serial killers

—to hide. Despite the gloom, the rising sun warmed the air relatively fast, and me along with it. I started to regret wearing the jacket.

The hike out to the falls would take about two hours, a long way from civilization, and a long way from help, which is why I brought my .44 Magnum. It should be big enough to stop a big cat.

If the killer was a mountain lion.

Of course, I had no reason not to believe otherwise. All evidence suggested it was. Big cat saliva? Okay, gross. But it should be an open and closed case. The instant a forensics report says "big cat saliva" and the bodies themselves (and I had seen the autopsy photos) showed every indication of an animal attack, then, yeah, I should have given the money back to Crystal. Except, of course, I had spent it. I really had needed it. Private investigators had a hard enough time finding work even *with* an office. No one would hire a homeless guy. And there was something else, right?

In fact, I pondered two *something elses...*

The wounds to the neck didn't look like big cat fangs to me. Sure, there had been claw marks in and around the wound, each digging deep into the flesh. Sure, I had fought gagging the entire time I'd examined the photos. But the actual wounds to the neck seemed—that is, the majority of the damage— seemed too small. In fact, the spacing between the fangs looked about the size of a human mouth. Not a big cat who could hyperextend its jaws. It might have been a smaller cat like a lynx, but such creatures had never been seen around here.

I had pointed that out to the sheriff, who sagely asked if I had ever seen animal wounds before? I hadn't, which led me to later Google a cheetah running down a gazelle. I watched closely as the cat closed its jaws around the poor creature's neck, crushing its windpipe. The kill fascinated me because the big cat didn't tear the creature's throat out. No, it had killed it... then went to work on its hindquarters, where all the meat was.

The second thing that stood out to me: the crime scene had little blood. The attack had taken place at a rockier section of ground near the stream that flowed from the pond at the base of the falls. The photographer had captured close-ups of bloody animal prints, which were damning indeed. I had asked if there was any indication that someone else had been there, and I could tell by the blank look on my ex-girlfriend's face that she hadn't even looked for prints from 'someone else.' Her people had looked for what they wanted to see: animal prints. As soon as they found one bloody paw print, it had given them enough evidence to confirm what they already wanted to believe. Granted, 99.9% of police forces in the country would have closed such a case, too, with that sort of evidence in light of the wounds on the bodies along with the saliva and paw prints.

I'd asked her about the lack of blood. A theory her office had floated was that the bodies might have been killed elsewhere, and perhaps a rival cat had dragged them to this spot where they'd been munched on. Indeed, large sections of the shoulders and thighs were missing from both of them. Lots of damage, but not a lot of blood at the crime scene. Hikers found the bodies early the next morning, hours after the attack, which the experts calculated had occurred around ten or so at night. No one had even reported Dana or Luke missing from the party. Forensics also didn't find any other signs of additional animal participation. As in, no coyotes or wolves or other critters gave the bodies a nibble.

To me, the scene looked too neat and tidy. No rocks dislodged, no deep grooves in the ground. Then again, the place was conveniently rocky, too. I noted blood smudges here and there in the photos. Not paw prints and not footprints nor handprints. Sheriff Waters suggested I quit acting like an idiot. I told her I was being paid to act like an idiot. Or to question everything. To me... I dunno, the blood smudges on the rocks looked like they had been rubbed. As if someone *had* left a footprint or boot print, and rubbed the blood to disguise them. Justine thought those smudges came from the victims struggling to get away from the cat.

The scene didn't offer any clear indication of a crime being committed, and the sheriff's office hadn't dug too deeply. That much was obvious. They accepted the big cat narrative, saw enough evidence to back said narrative up, and closed the case. Except there *had* been a witness. Sorta. An audio witness.

Crystal Bradbury had been on the phone with

her sister.

And no mountain lion had been heard. Not even a growl. Only her sister pleading for her life.

Who pleads with a big, silent cat?

I patted the reassuring weight under my armpit. It was a damn comforting feeling, knowing I packed some serious heat. I always carried my handgun with me when hiking in rough country. Thinking about two people being killed out here in these woods by god-knows-what made me more aware of it under my light jacket. I kept my zipper halfway down, and even practiced pulling the gun, quick-draw like. Alas, a cowboy I wasn't. Shoulder holsters didn't lend themselves to speed.

Minutes passed, and soon an hour, then another. I saw no sign of a big cat—or any more bodies on the winding trail. Nothing moved in the dense forest around me, which probably should have been eerie as hell, but wasn't. In fact, the woods seemed to give off the strangest feeling of security. It almost felt as though the plants and trees themselves telepathically said, *we got your back, bro.*

Okay, where did that come from?

Anyway, I spent the bulk of my time trying not to trip over exposed tree roots or jagged rocks. The trail varied from well-maintained to hardly visible. Luckily, I had my Rocky Mountain Trail App on my smartphone to keep me pointed in the right direction. And I had the memories of a teenage boy who had thoroughly partied in these woods, once upon a time. So many beers, and so many girls kissed.

Shortly before noon, I heard what I'd been waiting to hear: falling water.

The closer I got, the more thunderous the sound became. Yes, I knew I had a job to do, and yes, I knew that more than likely, a killer stalked these woods—even if said killer turned out to be a big cat —but once I heard the rush of falling water, the familiar draw pulled me onward. Indeed, I'd always been drawn to running water, beautiful, mysterious, and relaxing. I had been known to sit next to rivers or streams, watching the water for hours.

Then again, I also didn't have much of a life, either.

Once again, I was single. Sheriff Waters had decided she wanted something other than me for a man. In fact, a twenty-eight-year-old private detective who barely got by—and who lived in a one-bedroom apartment above his rundown office— probably wasn't what *any* girl truly pined for. I adored the freelance job and freelance lifestyle. Although it hurt like hell, I didn't blame her for bailing on me. Our dates at McDonald's, followed by Netflix at her place on her bigger TV, were marginal at best. I knew she'd felt consistently underwhelmed. Truth was, I had tried... hard. I liked that control-freak sheriff more than she realized. Loved? Who knows, maybe.

With a sigh, I stepped off the trail and headed over a leafy area that would lead to a breathtaking observation point. The closer I moved to the ledge, the more the leaves ahead of me thinned, revealing the magnificent waterfall. My heart thudded in my chest. I was, as always, transfixed by the sight of the rushing water falling through the air majestically. I stepped closer to the edge, a straight drop down a hundred feet or so to a churning pool below. Spray flew up into rainbows wherever the sunlight caught it, enchanting me all over again.

I took in a lot of air and closed my eyes, reveling in the sound of water, which seemed to emanate from the Earth itself. It smelled so damn good here. Clean, fresh, damp, perfect. I opened my eyes and watched the water falling and the drops of spray sparkling for many minutes.

So much power. So beautiful. So *right*.

Did everyone feel this way about water, or had I finally cracked? I didn't know, but as relaxing as I found this place, I still had a job to do. I reluctantly tore my gaze away from what amateur and professional photographers alike hiked hours to snap, what lovers idealized as the perfect romantic setting, and, apparently, where one killer stalked its prey, beast or otherwise.

Of course a beast, I thought. You saw the claw marks, the bloodied footpads. The forensics reports.

Yup, and something was still off. And I think Sheriff Waters knew it. I picked up on the way she wouldn't look me in the eye. She knew more than she let on, and didn't want to talk about it.

Or maybe she still kinda liked me.

Doubtful... but a guy could hope.

Chapter Four
A Little Out of the Way

I began a detailed inspection of the area.

Step by step, I looked up, down, and around, seeking anything that looked out of place in this verdant, clean forest. It took me ten minutes of searching, but I finally found a scrap of yellow police caution tape still tied to the branch of a bush, where it fluttered in the breeze like a dead butterfly's wing. The stark yellow movement hit me like a slap that knocked me from my profound admiration of this ethereal place and landed me right in the reality of the crime scene.

However, animal attacks didn't technically count as crime scenes. No one drags a cougar to trial for killing someone... unless we're talking about a fifty plus woman who still thinks she's thirty.

I stood back and took in the area, the rocky path cleaned, undoubtedly by the park service. Here, in this lovely place, two people had been killed. An uncountable number of innocent teens came here to party, to have their first kiss—and sometimes do more than that. I had some fond memories of this area, too. Kate O'Connor, in particular. My first kiss.

The fluttering yellow police tape once again dragged me out of my nostalgia. Sheriff Justine's people had left it behind after they'd collected all their evidence.

Speaking of evidence...

There had to be something they missed. What had the police, in their haste to wrap this case up, overlooked—either on purpose or by accident? The deaths happened about a week ago and this area saw a steady stream of hikers due to its popularity. However, it *did* take an ass-busting walk to get out here, so it didn't have *so* many visitors that the site would have been trampled.

A half dozen bouquets of flowers sat in a cluster nearby, but in the wrong place. Comparing the scene with the mental image I had of the photographs in the police report, I wandered around until recognizing the actual spot where the bodies had been discovered.

Whether or not a big cat had killed them, two people had lost their lives either here or near here. And Crystal had heard it all. For the next ten minutes, I made my way around that area, taking note of a dark spot in the dirt that could've been blood. The area had plenty of footprints, but one half-print stood out from the rest. Dress shoes... or at least *not* hiking boots. I fished out my cell phone and snapped a photo of it from several angles. No one in their right mind would come out here without hiking shoes—except for those vegan barefooter hippie types, but I did say *right* mind. I couldn't locate any other examples of a smooth-soled shoe. It could've been anything from a penny loafer to some thousand-dollar obscenity someone from the Founding Families would own. If it had any tread at all, a week's passing eroded it.

Even Dana and Luke, who'd been here for a party, had been wearing shoes appropriate for the deep woods. I pondered tracking down a list of attendees and asking them if anyone remembered seeing someone at the event wearing dress shoes. Some of the Founding Family crowd had their eccentricities, so I wouldn't put it past possible for an idiot to have come out here in a suit that cost more than my truck.

I searched in an outward-expanding spiral for any more signs of the mysterious shoeprints around the rocky clearing, noting many other footprints and scuff marks.

Some looked fresh, others not so much. Police and investigators, along with medical examiners, would have been swarming the area. Undoubtedly, they had tried not to contaminate the crime scene. Afterward, the place would have hosted numerous hikers and campers, many to come pay their respects. No telling how many had tromped through... certainly quite a few based on the amount of flowers.

The sun was hot on my neck. And yeah, I did regret wearing that jacket. Mosquitoes buzzed. In the background, the waterfall surged. The wind felt good on my face. I squatted often and sifted the dirt between my fingers, which always felt oddly comforting.

I came up with a simple theory: they hadn't been killed in this spot, and they hadn't been killed by a cougar. Sure, it appeared that way, which is why the case had been closed. But, hey, that's why I made the big bucks. And by big bucks, I mean the occasional retainer fee I receive. Emphasis on occasional.

Where they'd been killed, I hadn't a clue, but I decided to venture down one of the trails leading away from this spot. If my guess turned out to be true, there would be a location somewhere not terribly far from here, somewhere that had seen a real struggle, somewhere where a lot of blood had been spilled.

And what about the claw marks and cougar prints?

One thing at a time. Did I really think someone staged the death scene? For the moment, that made the most sense. I had to operate from that premise because part of me didn't buy the official story, and that part wanted to give Crystal *real* answers, not easy answers. Considering the amount of tissue missing from the bodies, there should have been an enormous amount of blood at the site where the bodies had been found. That thought reminded me of the hospital and the missing hemoglobin, and all the rumors about vampires in Shadow Pines.

Yeah, right. I'm sure we had a serial killer operating in the area who'd also heard those rumors and went out of his (or her, I suppose) way to capitalize on those rumors. A small town sheriff's department eyeball deep in bizarre stories of the supernatural would see something that looked like an honest-to-God vampire attack and just say 'nope, that didn't happen,' and look for easy answers. The feeling I got from Justine had been exactly that.

She'd said *nope* to this crime scene the way she'd have said *nope* to finding a dinner-plate sized spider perched on her toilet. More and more, the story of an animal attack didn't make sense... at least to me.

I wanted to know what the hell was going on in my woods.

Yes, my woods.

Just as much mine as anyone's, but this had been my stomping grounds for my entire life. The way most normal people had a fondness for their childhood home, I felt the same way toward the forest here.

Any private eyes worth their salt apprenticed with established investigators, learning the ropes, which I had done. Along with the required state training, my real education came when I had worked side-by-side with an old pro named Edward Jones. He'd taught me all he knew. While I hadn't gotten much use lately out of the considerable skills he'd passed on to me, that didn't mean I didn't know what I was doing.

That left me with a simple question: What would Jones do here?

I thought about that as I moved away from the scene, knowing my old mentor would tell me to look deeper, beyond the obvious. He would tell me to allow the clues to tell the story. So far, the clues told me that the two victims had died elsewhere, had bled out elsewhere. I was betting on that.

So I took in the surrounding trees and brush, the many ferns. The waterfall churned and crashed on my right as I moved down the path. I stopped often and paused to listen to it, my body veritably humming with life. I examined known campsites, now deserted, squatting on my heels and sifting through anything of interest, which didn't amount to much at all. How thoroughly Sheriff Waters and her team had gone over the area, I had no idea. Doubtful they had been *this* thorough. The bodies had been found, what, a hundred yards above me. Considering they'd all decided on a big cat before they even left the office in town, I had little faith they'd wandered more than twenty feet in any direction from where Dana and Luke had been found.

No one knew the route they'd taken away from

the party—or even the exact location of the party itself. From what Crystal said, it had been one of those creepy occultist type deals where everyone showed up wearing masks. They had food, drinks, possibly even participated in swinging or open sex, all under the guise of possibly-pretend mysticism. She didn't seem to know if any of the weirdo rich people honestly believed in any of the magical stuff or treated it like a game, or a secret society. In her opinion, Dana hadn't wanted to be involved with the swinging, and as soon as things devolved to sex, she'd taken Luke by the hand and left to show him the waterfall.

They'd told their friends and family that they'd gone for an overnight camp, the 'occult party' being all sorts of hush-hush. Crystal had gotten the truth, as she said Dana always told her everything. So I had some strange information to process.

There had been a party in the forest, late at night, with potential occult overtones.

People at said party had undoubtedly been drinking.

Most—if not all—of the attendees came from the upper classes.

At the time Dana and Luke walked off, the majority of partygoers would've been inebriated to some degree, and likely engaging in sexual acts— potentially with people they didn't recognize due to said masks.

Wow. Maybe Justine was right and I shouldn't have taken this case.

I also knew that their bodies had been found near the waterfall. Everyone came to see that... which made me think that the killer had purpose-fully put them there *knowing* they would be found, and soon. That didn't make a lot of sense to me. Most killers bend over backward to hide the bodies as long as possible. Every day that passes after the death makes it more difficult to gather evidence that could lead to a conviction. So, why would the killer *want* the bodies found? To send a message, most likely. But why make it look like an animal attack if they wanted to send a message?

Hmm. I'd need to think about that. First, I had to find the actual murder site. If I could do that, I'd have something to take back to Crystal, maybe even share with Justine.

A number of trails spread away from the falls. I didn't really know the exact location of the party, but I could guess based on my knowledge of a few clearings in the area large enough to host such a gathering. If Dana or Luke had used an exercise app, we could have traced their exact path. No such luck, according to the police report. But then again, they hadn't been out here for a healthy hike.

I checked my phone. My app was turned on... but no one gave a shit where I wandered off to.

Where's the world's smallest violin when you need it?

I continued down the trail...

Chapter Five
The Case is a Breeze

Crystal seemed confident she had heard the waterfall in the background.

Consequently, I never ventured past where the sound of crashing water fell silent. A half-dozen trails crisscrossed the area, and I spent the better part of the day wandering over them, encountering two hikers in the process. I wanted to tell them to beat it, to not dare trample on a potential crime scene, but I only smiled and munched on my peanut butter and honey sandwich.

As I watched them go, I took in a lot of air, held it in my lungs, exhaled.

A powerful gust of wind swept through the forest and rattled the trees around me. Yes, I loved the water—water of all types, really: oceans and rivers, streams and the rain. I loved the rain most of all. Hell, I even loved the sound of kitschy zen-type desk fountains.

But the wind held a special place in my heart, too. I'd always loved the sound of it whistling through branches overhead, or thundering over my ears. Others hid from windstorms, but I never did. I enjoyed walking in them, feeling the raw power, observing its dominion over everything. The strongest trees bowed. I once had someone tell me he believed the wind stole his soul. I believe he couldn't have been more wrong. The wind gave life. Hell, the wind *was* life.

The breath of God.

Then again, I always was a little weird.

I stood there upon a side trail not far from where two people had met their maker and listened to this sudden gust of wind that seemed to be blowing everywhere at once, swaying the massive treetops above and rustling pine needles along the forest floor. I closed my eyes and felt it move over me, through my hair, thunder over my ears. With the waterfall cascading nearby and the gusting wind blasting everywhere, this place felt like heaven.

When I closed my eyes, the wind seemed to pick up strength. I reveled in the sensation of it on my skin and in my hair, briefly forgetting why I'd come here. I lifted my hands and the wind increased as if in response. It had to be up to gale-force now, easily forty or fifty miles an hour. Dirt and debris pelted me, but I ignored it.

When I lowered my hands, the wind died. I

could almost believe I'd become the forest's maestro, controlling the symphonic orchestra of nature. I *almost* believed. I wasn't delusional, just someone who appreciated nature... perhaps a little too much.

While standing there with my hands down at my sides, I became all too aware that the wind had completely died.

And because I was weird—and because I'd spent far too much time alone with my imagination while waiting for cheating spouses to emerge from seedy hotels—I raised my hands again, imagining that I could control the wind.

The breeze stirred, picking up.

I wasn't delusional. Obviously, it was a coincidence that the wind had died down when I lowered my hands, and started up again when I raised them. The wind could do that. A fickle friend. And, like the rain, I was always sad to see it go.

Except... well, something happened as I raised my hands higher.

The wind intensified more.

Coincidence? Of course, but it was fun to pretend nonetheless. I was like a kid running around the neighborhood with his arms outstretched, thinking that at any moment now he was going to lift off and fly like Superman.

I lowered my hands and, coincidentally again, the wind stopped, too.

Weird, I thought, and almost went back to searching the many trails.

Except something had come over me.

A sense of excitement.

I couldn't focus on the crime scene. In fact, I'd nearly forgotten about it entirely.

Two people had been killed. Near this spot. Other than a sister listening on a phone, there hadn't been witnesses, but that wasn't true, was it?

No. Not true at all.

Nature was here. The trees, animals, the Earth itself as well. The waterfall had towered over everything. They say when someone dies, that the tragic event is forever imprinted at that spot on the land, to replay itself over and over for those sensitive enough to 'see' it.

I, of course, wasn't sensitive enough to see such things. Hell, I'd never even seen a ghost—and never wanted to, either. Plenty of stories of ghosts circulated around Shadow Pines, enough to where even the skeptics among us would never outright say that ghosts didn't exist. The hard-headed ones would always deflect with something like saying they hadn't yet seen enough to completely convince them. Often, it was the doubters who would return with their own first-hand accounts of hauntings, real fear and excitement in their eyes, ghost stories of their own. Shadow Pines had that effect on people: turning skeptics into believers.

My family had been lucky... the house I'd grown up in didn't have any ghosts. If you asked most people around town, that made us the exception. My office, too. Never had anything unexplainable happen there... except a landlord who magically appeared in person whenever the rent was late. Luckily, he worked with me. He kinda had to, which is probably why he didn't like me much. Not like he had a stack of people lined up to rent my space. If he kicked me out, he'd have an empty building for months if not years. *Some* chance of getting rent beat no chance at all.

But the thought that something beyond the human experience existed, intrigued me, and I couldn't quite shake it. Maybe that's why I stayed around this crazy town. But somewhere along the line, I'd become Schrodinger's skeptic. I simultaneously wanted to believe in that stuff but also didn't want to. The reality of it would be too unnerving. I much preferred a world I could explain in rational terms, but remained fascinated by the what-ifs of the beyond.

Of course, my old mentor would have been disappointed in me. He didn't believe in the supernatural. He believed in facts that would hold up in a court of law.

I stood with my hands down by my sides, waiting for the wind to pick up again on its own and prove I'd been pretending. The air remained still. The scent of moist soil, aromatic cedars and pines, and the sweet grass surrounded me. Other than the cascading waterfall, I heard nothing. The wind that had been blowing so powerfully mere seconds earlier had become a memory. Perhaps I had only imagined it.

Perhaps...

Or perhaps not.

And so, I raised my hands. As a cold shiver swept through me, the wind appeared, rustling the forest. It built into a howl around me, over me... but despite its apparent ferocity, I felt only a mild breeze against my face.

"What the...?"

I raised my hands higher and higher, and the wind roared faster and faster. As I stretched my arms out over my head, the treetops bent almost horizontally. Branches cracked and crashed throughout the forest.

"My God," I whispered... but the howling wind swallowed the sound of my voice.

I lowered my hands and the wind died down.

"I'm dreaming."

Indeed, I would have chalked it up to my over-active imagination except for one thing: hundreds of broken branches littered the ground at my feet. Clear evidence that a mini hurricane had occurred. One of the branches caught my eye...

Resting on the ground a few feet away lay a tree branch stained in blood.

Chapter Six
Sanity Check

Ron Moore sat across from me at the Pine Stump Cafe, drinking beer from the bottle and watching a group of boisterous high school students playing pool.

"Were we ever that obnoxious, Max?" he asked. "When we were in high school."

"More obnoxious, I think," I said.

My best friend drank more beer and shook his head. "We had more to laugh about, I guess. These kids today, they're growing up in a different Shadow Pines. A dangerous Shadow Pines."

Ron had a right to be cynical. Three years ago, Ron's wife, Daphne, had been killed in—you guessed it—an animal attack. Except it had occurred while she was jogging along the streets of her residential neighborhood, her normal route. Ron had led a search for the creature and had returned with a dead cougar... a particularly *big* dead cougar. It had been shot multiple times, prompting many in the community to predict that the animal attacks would finally now stop.

And they had... until now. Now, I worried the local mountain lion community would face a harsh backlash they didn't deserve. Meanwhile, Ron coped with his loss as best he could. I knew he often drank to deal with things. Hell, I would have, too. I missed Daphne more than I let on. She was a true friend. She didn't deserve what had happened to her. None of the victims around here did. It got me wondering how many of these 'animal attacks' had really been the work of the same killer who'd claimed Dana and Luke.

After Ron drained his first draft and motioned for another, he looked at me. "So what's up? You sounded upset on the phone."

Ron would know. We'd been friends our whole lives. Met in first grade, hung out together all the time as kids. We played football from pee-wee all the way up through high school. I was the best man at his wedding and a pallbearer for his wife's funeral.

"That would be an understatement."

"What the devil does that mean?" he asked.

"Good choice of words."

Ron stared at me. He was a big guy, which is why he played offensive line in football. I wasn't quite as big, which is why I played tight end. That, and I could catch a football with my *hands*. Ron more often tried to catch one with his chin. Finally, he raised a bushy eyebrow and asked, "Am I missing something here?"

For an answer, I opened my hand, palm upward. I had been practicing the movement since returning from the woods. I'd discovered that my palm had to be faced upward; additionally, I had to raise my hand slowly. And if I raised both hands together, I got a stronger reaction. At present, I lifted only the one.

His shirt began flapping. The little square napkin sitting before him fluttered... then went flying.

"Jesus," said Ron, looking over his shoulder, already sounding a bit drunk. "Would someone close the goddamn door?"

Except the doors *were* closed, both front and back. And still the wind continued, clinking the wine glasses that hung upside down in the rack overhead. Napkins, receipts, and straws scuttled over the scarred wooden bar. Ron's shirt flapped wildly and so did his thinning hair. Nearby, balls rolled and clacked around the pool tables. A waitress carrying drinks reached down with her free hand to hold her skirt in place.

"What the hell's going on?" asked Ron, turning in his seat. "Where's that blasted wind coming from?"

He looked up for a ceiling fan that wasn't there. Then he looked at me. As he did, I lowered my right hand, and the lower it got, the more the wind subsided.

Ron didn't put two and two together yet. Not at first. After all, why would he?

"It's coming from me, Ron."

He snorted. "Now *that* I could believe."

Crude humor aside, I made a show of raising my hand again and the wind increased, flapping his shirt around his big frame. I lowered it again, and the wind decreased. Eyes wide, Ron couldn't help but do the math. Then he broke out into a wide grin.

"Ha, that's a cool trick. You almost had me going there. Is someone controlling the AC?" He turned in his seat, looked for someone standing near a thermostat, except neither of us knew where to look. "Well, they're somewhere."

"It's no trick, Ron."

"You having someone film me? Is this going on some YouTube practical joke channel? Is that how you're making money, now that your business has all but dried up?"

"First of all no, and second, ouch. I happen to have a client."

"A *paying* client?"

"Of course."

"Fine. So tell me how you did that wind trick."

"It's not a trick, and there's no one controlling the AC or opening and closing doors or standing behind you with a giant fan."

"Fine." He squinted his reddish eyes at me. "Then do it again."

For the first time in many hours, I grinned. After

all, this had been a helluva weird day.

I took in some air and raised both hands, palms up. I did so with the intent to cause a bigger storm. *Intent* seemed to be the most important part.

Wind erupted seemingly everywhere at once, but I knew, in fact, it was blowing *away* from me, in all directions. I was in a sort of wind-free vortex. Around me, everything moved. Glasses shot off tables, menus erupted from storage bins like flocks of startled seagulls. A bad toupee flapped free, and hamburger buns went flying. Ron reached out, fighting the wind, and pulled my hands down. The wind slowed, then stopped as my hands came to rest on the table top. The restaurant devolved into turmoil, people standing, running, chattering, wiping spilled drinks and flying food from their clothing. Neon signs had fallen from wall mounts, and glasses and dishes had flown off tables. Napkins still fluttered in the air like so many butterflies.

Ron ignored it all; instead, he stared at me. "Holy sweet mother of God."

"Exactly."

"Max, what... *was* that? Please say it was a trick."

"No trick."

"Wh-where's the camera?"

"There's no camera, my friend. This is real."

"You... you did that?"

"Would you like another demonstration?"

He said nothing, and so I raised one hand with

the intent to whirl some wind around his head, and that's exactly what happened. The look of fear and awe on my friend's face was priceless.

"Okay, stop. Jesus, Max."

"I'm not Jesus. At least, I don't think I am."

"What's happening?"

"No clue. But I needed you to see it, too. At least I know it's not all in my head."

"It's a miracle. Wait, there are no cameras on me, right? Swear to God this is true."

"It's true buddy. Something is happening to me."

"If this is some trick, I swear to God I will get you back every day for the rest of my life."

I laughed and was about to answer, when I noticed a man at the far end of the counter staring at me. He had Hollywood hair and wore a leather jacket. Late June was way too warm for a leather jacket. Over the years, I'd seen him around town here and there, although we never spoke. Small towns were like that. You could see some people nearly every day and never speak to them once in years. Most people who lived in bigger cities thought all small town folk know each other. Sure, we might recognize each other, and we might even nod and say hello, but we certainly don't know everyone's business. Anyway, I wasn't casually friendly with this guy, although I saw him often enough... and usually at night. At the bars, in fact, of which Shadow Pines had about five or six. Anyway, you would think if you'd seen someone a few dozen times, you would eventually nod or say hi. But this guy never gave me an opening, and years ago, I'd quit looking for one. Who he was, I hadn't a clue. What he did for a living, I didn't know that either. But he had nice hair.

It stood out to me at the moment that the guy had taken a sudden keen interest in me; in fact, I caught him looking over at us two or three times. Perhaps most interesting, the blowing wind didn't seem to bother him, unlike everyone else in the cafe, who all still looked around and chattered excitedly about the bizarre wind.

As if my being able to summon wind hadn't been the weirdest thing I experienced, I had the distinct impression that despite him sitting all the way at the far end of the bar, he somehow listened to us.

Impossible, I knew. Then again, so was controlling the wind.

"C'mon," I said. "Let's walk, I'll tell you outside."

"Yeah, no shit. This place is a mess anyway."

I laughed, and left some money on the table.

On the way out, stepping over some broken glass, I discreetly shoved a few twenties in the tip jar on the bar, which was presently being tended to by a befuddled Reggie Smith, owner of the Pine Stump Cafe.

Chapter Seven
The Internet Has Everything

I spent a good long while pacing around my apartment.

Ron had gone home, probably to drink the night away. Truth was, I felt like finishing a bottle or two myself. Except getting drunk wouldn't make this problem go away.

Was it a problem?

"Yes," I said to no one. "It was."

Then again, I thought, as I wandered aimlessly in front of my worn-out couch, it was kind of fun to see Ron's surprise. And to see the reactions of everyone in the cafe. Except for the one bloke who didn't much react at all.

Fun or not, something very weird was going on. Yes, I lived in Shadow Pines where the bizarre had become commonplace, but I had always seemed to exist outside of all that... drama. On the fringe of weird, not immersed in it. My life had always been decidedly *not weird*, and I liked it that way. No, I preferred it that way.

I raised my upturned palm and a swirling gust of wind circled my simple dwelling.

"Welcome to Weirdsville," I said.

I took in some air, held it, and paused on my way into the kitchen and that first of many beers. "Why wind?" I ask myself out of the blue. "I mean, what was the deal with that?"

For an answer, I did the only thing I could think of.

I fired up my laptop.

***

I poked around on the Internet for a bit and stumbled across various chatrooms with people claiming to control the wind with their mind. I mean... really? That's a thing? And who was I to say otherwise?

I pinched myself again, for the dozenth time.

Not dreaming. Unless I dreamed I pinched myself.

I read many of their experiences, but none sounded like mine, or how I went about controlling the wind with my upturned palms and intention. As an experiment, I focused on creating the wind in my mind only, and mustered a slight breeze. Hardly anything at all, actually. But the moment I brought my upturned palms into play—whammo—a burst of wind blew the dining table chair over next to me.

More digging, more reading. I ended up in the 'strange shit' section of YouTube. I watched a lot of people standing around fields, 'controlling' the wind with their minds, pointing to swaying tree branches as evidence.

After some more online searching, I headed to Amazon and settled on a book called *The Elementals: Earth, Wind, Fire and Water.*

Elementals. It was a word I'd come across a number of times now in the last hour of being on the net. I waited for it to download to my Kindle, then settled into a nook on my battered and abused couch... and read until my eyes hurt.

According to the book, Elementals were four nature spirits that embodied the elements of antiquity. The embodiments—or incarnations—of these elements took on the characteristics of the elements. In fact, Shakespeare's *The Tempest* was about a wind Elemental who aided the main character. According to legend, Elementals, often under the guidance of archangels, were responsible for creating, renewing, protecting and sustaining life.

I read well into the night... and finished the book. Argh.

More. I needed more information.

Back on the computer. More research. Found a blog of interest. According to the writer—who claimed he was quite sensitive to the spirit world and wrote from firsthand experience—Elementals came in all shapes and sizes. Often they were as elusive as spirits, existing just beyond our earthly sensitivities, but sometimes, not so much. Sometimes, Elementals could manifest through humans, too.

I read every blog the guy wrote—dozens of them. I got up and rubbed my eyes, paced.

Elementals could manifest in humans? I just so happened to be human, and I could do this: I raised my hand, and a small wind blasted around my small apartment, knocking over a lava lamp, nearly breaking it in the process.

Oops.

I picked up the lamp and continued pacing. I truly didn't know what to do or who to turn to for help. Only that blog seemed to contain any kind of useful information. Wait, the author had a contact page. I hurried back to my laptop and dashed off a long, rambling, slightly incoherent email that I sent via one of my dummy email accounts. (All private eyes have dummy email accounts.) If that guy could make heads or tails of my email, then he had to be a psychic indeed.

Another beer in hand—a cold one from the fridge—I dropped down into my overstuffed recliner. I'd gotten about halfway through it when a *ping* came from my computer.

Chapter Eight
Imagining Things

I paced in my apartment, waiting for the phone to ring when someone knocked on the office door downstairs.

As far as I could remember, I didn't have an appointment today, nor was I expecting anyone. Technically, I should still be in the office, as it was just before 6 p.m. Then again, technically, I shouldn't have been able to control the wind either. Things change.

The knocking came again, this time more urgently.

I made a living out of following cheaters and, occasionally, catching bad guys. Hell, I'd even sent my share of criminals to jail. Which was why private eyes kept guns around; after all, anyone who did this job long enough would certainly make a handful of enemies, ones highly prone to being more than a little vindictive.

It's also why I had installed a cheap camera in a shadowy nook above my office door. Always a damn good idea to see who came pounding at your office door at all hours of the night. Anyway, I swiped on my phone, pulled up my security app, and opened a live feed of my office door downstairs.

The man standing there was a handsome devil: black hair, slender build... and a lot of attitude. He wore a leather jacket, jeans, boots. Looked a bit like an old-school greaser. I'd seen him around town a few times. Okay, more than a few. Sometimes, I'd run into him drinking at the Pines Café, hanging around some of the college kids, although he looked a little older than college. But that could have been the confident, cocky manner in which he held himself. Either way, he radiated trouble, and I wasn't in the mood for any trouble.

His features were a bit hard to make out in the video feed, which was weird, since I'd gotten high def. I squinted, trying to see the problem. His face was... blurry, not sharp, smudged even. Like someone had filled him in with crayons, rather than actual skin. I shook my head, dismissed it...

Wait... what was that spot on his cheek? I took a screen shot of it, blew the image up. No, it wasn't a spot. It was... well, nothing.

Nothing at all.

Or maybe a hole, or an empty spot.

A hole or empty spot in his face. In fact, I was certain I could see *through* his face. Yes, I recognized my office window on the other side, where his cheek should be. I rubbed my eyes, and noticed a similar blank spot in his neck... and, my God, where were his hands? Confused, I went back to the live feed. As he knocked again, I saw... nothing at the end of his sleeve. Nothing at all. Like his hands had been perfectly camouflaged with his surroundings. Or he didn't have hands, and knocked with his stumpy wrists.

The knocking continued, and on the video, the end of the jacket sleeve stopped six inches or so from the door, where it would be if someone who possessed hands rapped their knuckles on my door. He didn't have hands. Yet the physical knock reverberated through the quiet evening.

He paused and sort of cocked his head, as if listening. My apartment was located directly above my office. Few people knew that, especially since the apartment was leased in my mother's maiden name, God rest her soul. Private eyes, after all, need anonymity. But I also liked to keep a close watch on my office. It was often very telling who came sniffing around.

So, I stayed quiet, although there was no way in hell he could hear me in my apartment one floor above. Still, trouble sort of... radiated from him in a way that surprised me. It was almost as if I could feel his darkened energy, but that had to be paranoia on my part.

Right?

Wait. I could *feel* his darkened energy?

Where the hell had that hippie shit come from?

Anyway, after half a minute of listening, he gave up and started to walk away, but spotted the camera above. He cocked his head a little and smiled, and I was certain, damn certain, he had no teeth... and I could see straight through his mouth out the back of his head to the street. What the hell was going on? When he finished smiling like a creep, he continued on down the street and disappeared out of view. The scuff of boots disappeared shortly after that. I half expected to hear a knock at my apartment door, but it never came.

A minute later, the phone rang, and I nearly jumped out of my skin.

"Is this Max Long?" asked a voice on the other end.

"It is."

"This is Michael, you emailed me yesterday about my blog."

"Actually, this morning. Early this morning." I paused to compose myself. "I'm sure I sounded insane in my email. Hell, I *feel* insane—"

"Just relax, Max. I don't think you're insane."

Michael had a soft, comforting voice, one that calmed my nerves—nerves that had been on edge all day, made worse by that creep at my office door.

"Let's just say the jury is still out," I said. I mean, did I really see through that guy knocking at my door? Surely it had to be a trick with the camera, an error in the feed, a glitch in the compression.

He laughed softly. "Max, I'd like to ask you a few questions. Would that be okay?"

"If it helps me understand what's happening to me, then ask away."

He chuckled again, then got to it. "Would you say you've had an affinity for wind all your life?"

At least he started with an easy one. I nodded. "Definitely."

"Would you also say you have a similar affinity for water? As in, do both elements calm you, yet also make you feel alive? Do both somehow resonate deeply within you?"

"Yes, but isn't that the case for every—"

"How about fire, Max? Do you ever find yourself enchanted by fire? Nearly hypnotized?"

"Doesn't everyone?"

"No, Max. Not everyone. Last question: do you enjoy walks in nature? Hiking, camping, backpacking? Do you have, say, a garden at home?"

I thought of the little herbal garden on my balcony—the same one that Ron mercilessly ridiculed. I thought of my many weekend hikes and once-a-month camping trips.

"Yes to everything," I said.

"A resounding yes?"

"Yes. Now, what's your point?"

"Max, would you be open to meeting me?"

"Sure."

"And giving me a, umm, demonstration."

"Like I said, if it helps me understand what's happening to me, I'll do anything."

Chapter Nine
The Blogger

We met at a little coffee shop named 'Latte Morning' in downtown Shadow Pines early the next morning.

Turned out Michael lived just a few hours away and had been driving since a little after 5 a.m. He didn't at all look like I expected. In fact, he reminded me of George Costanza. I had already given him a small demonstration of my wind-making talents—by blowing off a napkin at a nearby table —and he seemed suitably impressed. Floored, even. He asked if I could make fire, too, and I told him I hadn't tried. Or even thought of it. I told him wrapping my brain around this wind business had been traumatizing enough. He smiled, reached inside his pocket, and pulled out a small matchbox. With a practiced flick, he slid the cover open, then removed a single match. Great, the guy's a stage magician.

"Can you light this, Max?"

"Anyone can light a match."

"I'm not asking you to light it in the usual manner. With your mind, Max. And be careful. Don't burn this place to the ground."

"I don't know what I'm doing, and I feel ridiculous."

"Says the guy who just blew a napkin off a table from halfway across the cafe. Just focus, and scale it down. I happen to like my fingers."

I did as I was told, applying the same sense of intention to my thoughts, except nothing happened. Raising my hand did nothing either.

"Try snapping your fingers," said Michael.

I did, and the match flared brightly.

Michael jumped, and quickly shook it out. "My, my, my. I never thought I would see another person with the gift in the flesh."

"Another what?"

"Elemental," he said.

Of course, I had read all about elementals, which is how I'd ended up on Michael's blog site. But that didn't stop my mouth from dropping. After all, I had witnessed the matchstick igniting too. And I'd been practicing my wind storms all night, unaware that another type of manifestation—fire— was waiting within me as well.

"What is happening to me?" I asked.

"I take it you didn't read my book?"

"I got excited and emailed you after I'd read the blogs."

The little man pushed up his glasses. "Understandable. Then let me fill you in on what you missed. There are many of us with the potential to be elementals. Love for nature is within most humans. A deep and spiritual connection to nature is another thing altogether. Such people are candidates to be chosen..."

"Er, chosen by whom?"

"You tell me. Were you approached by anybody?"

"No."

"Did you dream of anybody?"

"Not that I recall."

"Did anything out of the ordinary happen to you in the past few days?"

I thought about it. "I did feel funny after seeing the meteor."

"What meteor?"

"The one from last week. The one that, you know, blazed across the sky. Anyone could see it." I narrowed my eyes. Come to think of it, the meteor likely happened around the same time Crystal's sister died.

"That's it!" he said. "Did you see where this meteor landed?"

"No, and I'm not sure it landed. It just, you know, came and went. Streaked across the sky."

"Max, did anyone else see the meteor?"

"Um... I haven't asked, but the news didn't

mention it."

"Doesn't matter. I doubt they reported it. The meteor was both a portent of things to come... and an activation within you."

"Activation?"

"Your abilities were dormant. Now, not so much. The meteor is the key. Hold on."

He pulled out his phone and feverishly swiped his fingers across the screen. I looked around at the cute little coffee shop. It was no Starbucks, but people here liked it that way.

"Just as I thought, Max. There's no mention of a meteor in this area by anyone. Apparently, you were the only one to see it, although I suspect that may not be entirely accurate."

"What do you mean?"

"Others probably saw it as well, those who needed to see it." the little man nodded. "Yes, I've heard of such meteors. Legend has it they are also a warning for the monsters among us to flee... or to clean up their act."

"Monsters among us?"

"You missed a lot in my book, Max. There's a theory about elementals; in particular, about their sudden presence in a place. The theory goes like this: Nature likes order. Nature likes the natural, as she intended things to be. Life and death are natural, for instance. If something breaks the natural order of things, Nature herself will seek to correct the disorder."

"What could break the natural order of things?"

I asked.

"Think, Max. What is the one pervasive legend that surrounds this area? I live two hours away, and even I have heard the stories surrounding Shadow Pines."

"Vampires." I said.

"Exactly, Max. Creatures who live outside of nature, abominations that thumb their noses at the natural order of things."

"But vampires aren't real. They're only stories told over campfires."

"Max, I have looked into such things. I have studied such things. I have had witnesses contact my blog about all manner of the paranormal. I can assure you, vampires are real, and they're here in Shadow Pines, and they have been here for some time. Your disproportionate amount of murders and disappearances should be evidence enough. Shadow Pines also generates its fair share of vampire stories, hence why you had the answer readily available. Max, most towns don't have a history of vampire stories… and other unexplained goings-on. They just don't. Shadow Pines does. Why do you think so many documentaries are filmed here? Shadow Pines is a hotbed of paranormal activity... and not the nice kind."

"There are nice kinds?"

"The occasional UFO sighting. The occasional Bigfoot sightings. Ghosts here and there. Maybe a lake monster or two. Not straight up murder. Not people with whole nights blocked form their memories, which is a common occurrence in this town—and which is known to be a hallmark of an active vampire community. Weren't two hikers killed just last week?"

"An animal attack," I said. "And they weren't exactly hikers… though a lot of people who go hiking around here are never heard from again."

"Uh huh. Another animal attack in Shadow Pines. Big surprise, Max. How many more people are going to be killed before you realize that here be monsters?"

"I don't know how to answer that question."

"Luckily, you don't have to. Nature did it for you. She brought forth an answer to the unnatural problems plaguing this town, and that answer is you, Max."

"Crap." I gazed up at the ceiling. "Then this town's in trouble."

Chapter Ten
Nature Boy

I needed some air.

In truth, I always preferred the outdoors. Must be that one-of-a-kind connection I had with nature and all. Anyway, I pushed the coffee shop's door aside and stepped out for some fresh air with Michael trailing behind me. My head buzzed. Like seriously buzzed, so much so that I doubted it came from the mocha latte. I said as much to Michael.

"You're tuning into Nature, Max," said Michael.

He fell in step beside me as we strolled down the street into town. Admittedly, I kept an eye out for the guy who came a-knocking last night. Had he been a vampire? I mean... what was the deal with his hands, or lack thereof?

"What, exactly, does that mean?" I asked.

"Tuning in with Nature?"

"Max, think of yourself as an extension of Nature... a very important extension. And think of yourself as having woken up from a very long sleep —"

"Except I feel like I'm dreaming *now*."

"On the contrary, Max. You have been sleep-walking through life, until now."

"Until the meteor's arrival."

"Other factors, too. There are some elementals who never awaken."

"Why is that?"

"They are not needed, most likely."

"So Mother Nature peppers the Earth with potential elementals... just in case?"

Michael shrugged. "Hard to say, Max. But there is evidence that Elementals are basically regular humans—albeit people who are in touch with nature —waking up to find himself or herself being used as a tool... or a weapon. Perhaps, in this case, an assassin. Nature's assassin."

"First of all, I'm not a killer. I'm just a private eye, and not a very successful one."

"I suspect you are an honest man. A good man. A moral man. Hey, follow me."

He gave my sleeve a tug and I turned off the somewhat busy sidewalk and into an alley. He led me deeper within... all the way down to a dumpster sandwiched between a bar and the town's only grocery store. The alley was surprisingly ominous for a small town. I'd heard of drug deals going down here, and, yes, a body or two had shown up in that very dumpster. We weren't the unofficial murder capital of the state for nothing.

A warm wind swept down the narrow corridor, bringing it with the smell of slightly rotten food and not-so-rotten beer. Mostly, though, the wind felt good, and my body tingled from head to toe. That old feeling of longing returned, that feeling that I was somehow separated from... a place I needed to be. A sense that I had been missing *something* overwhelmed me, like I'd been a twin in the womb, but my brother never made it, a connection forever lost.

Michael opened the dumpster lid and peered inside, then nodded to himself.

"It's mostly empty, just some cardboard." He scanned the immediate surroundings. "All brick in the alleyway. Nothing should catch on fire."

"Say again?"

But he ignored my question. "We're pretty deep in the alley. Not a lot of foot traffic. I think this is the spot."

"The spot for what?"

"Why, to practice."

"Practice what, exactly?"

"Max, I don't think you realize that you've painted a target on your back last night. That little wind demonstration at the bar didn't go unnoticed by your enemies."

"I don't have enemies."

"You do now. The guy who came knocking?

The guy with no hands? He is almost assuredly a vampire. And he didn't show up to hire you."

I swallowed. "How... how do you know he was a vampire?"

"Because vampires don't show up on film, in mirrors, or on camera."

"But parts of him did..."

"Makeup, Max. He was wearing makeup... everywhere but his hands."

"But why is he looking for me?"

"Why indeed, Max? A social visit... or was he going to fix a potential problem?"

"Fix a problem?"

"You, Max. You're his problem. You're about to be all of their problems. Which is why we need to get you up to speed on who you really are. And before you ask, you're an elementalist, Max. You have been given access to elemental forces, and the vampires are not happy. Now, are you ready for your training?"

And train we did...

With Michael's help, I learned how to summon fire and rain, and to shake the ground. Not too much shaking. Just enough to rattle the dumpster. I both started fires and rained them out, all while wind whipped faster and faster down the alley, howling like a living thing, which I'd come to believe it kinda sorta was. All the while, I stood there with my hands out and my eyes closed, looking very much like something out of a Harry Potter movie.

As I worked on forming a ball of fire, noise

arose in the distance. Voices, I think. No, whispers. Either way, they were so faint that I could have been imagining them. Try as I might, I couldn't make out the words.

"Do you hear that?" I asked, just as I doused the latest fire with a mini rainstorm, complete with mini thunderclouds. I thought it to be actually quite cute. With a wave of my hand, the clouds dispersed in a burst of rain. "Voices. On the wind."

"Ah. You are hearing nature itself, Max."

"I don't understand."

"It is all of life that surrounds you, from the critters in this alley, to the great oaks that stand outside of town. It is the birds in the air and insects everywhere. All are here to aid you."

"To help me fight the vampires?"

"In a nutshell, yes."

"And I'm here to do what, destroy them?"

"No, Max. You are here to restore balance."

"I'm just one man," I said.

"One man who has nature on his side. Now, why don't we take this outside the city? Do you happen to know of somewhere we could go for some privacy? Perhaps an old cabin or something no one would miss?"

I didn't have to think long. "Yeah... there's a spot with an abandoned shack. Been there for years."

"Perfect." Michael clapped.

***

It sat about three miles outside town, a little ways off the beaten track.

I'd seen it on many a hike; interestingly, I often wondered what it would look like to watch it burn. Such thoughts had concerned me at the time. Now, I sorta understood where they had come from. Either that, or I am a natural pyro.

With the coast clear, I alternately set fire to the shack, then doused it with rain water. More than once, I found myself staring in awe at the fire... or at the mini rain clouds. That I did all of this from powers inside of me went well beyond anything I could imagine.

"Good," Michael said after my latest round of fire and water. "Again."

I did it over and over until I mastered all forms of making fire... from smaller flames that could light a cigarette, to fiery winds that could level forests or buildings. I also learned I could change water to ice and back as well as manipulate the ground at my feet, raising stones from the earth or even shaping columns of rock.

When the shack had finally burned to the ground and Michael and I stood together under a localized thunderstorm, dripping wet from the pouring rain, I turned to Michael and said, "I'm not dreaming, am I?"

"No, Max."

"This is really happening?"

He nodded. "You have been given great gifts,

Max. Use them wisely."

"But how do I use them? You said to restore balance... what does that mean?"

"There is no easy answer, Max," said Michael, as the storm continued drenching the burned-out shack... and us. "You will have to use great care and wisdom."

"Does Nature realize that I'm just a normal guy?"

"Normal guys are part of nature, too, Max." He paused, rain dripping from his nose. "Let me suggest this: on some level, you very much wanted to be here, in this place and time, to restore order, to do what you can to right a great wrong."

"And vampires are a great wrong?"

"Some, not all."

"What if I ignore these gifts?"

"Then I expect they will fade away... that is, if the vampires let you live. Remember, you are very much on their radar."

"And we're certain vampires are real?" I asked.

"I guess you are about to find out. At least, you are equipped to handle them now."

"By unleashing fire and lightning and rain upon their heads?"

"In a word, yes. And anything else within nature at your disposal. There is a reason why elementals are used to restore balance. They are literally a force of nature. Some might even say unstoppable."

"Me, unstoppable?"

"Yes, Max. Think about it... you can level towns

with fire, floods, earthquakes and storms. You think one vampire—or even a host of them—could match your power?"

"Maybe not, but if they are as devious as you say they are, they might find other ways to attack me."

"Are some clever? Definitely. Will some seek to outwit you? You can bet on it. But correct me if I'm wrong, don't most private investigators have some sense of street smarts? Some sense of taking care of themselves? Not to mention having seen the seedier side of life. I am sure you have a few tricks up your sleeve, along with your newfound powers."

"My last case was looking for a lost labradoodle."

"Did you find it?"

"I did."

"Thus employing your street smarts and tenacity."

Hmm. The poor little guy had been dognapped by the woman's ex-boyfriend. A series of clues and hunches had led me to the critter being kept in Spencer Heights, a good ways south of here, at an RV in a trailer park. I had kicked a little ass breaking into that RV. Street smarts? Toughness? Hard to say. But yeah, I guess I could take care of myself. And with these new skills... maybe I could take on the undead... if they really existed.

I thought of the young man who had shown up at my office door last night, the young man whose face I could see *through*, and who sported invisible hands. Yeah, that defied any explanation I could come up with in the rational universe. I had never encountered anything like that before... at least that I remembered. Could vampires be real? I didn't know, but 'hollow man' at my door offered pretty damning evidence. Perhaps I should investigate the guy.

"I can say with certainty that the vampires will be coming for you, Max."

"Well, that's just great. There's always a string attached, isn't there?"

He nodded, then studied me. "Perhaps I should tell you a thing or two about vampires."

We headed back to town, stopping at Pedro's. I'd been going to that Mexican restaurant since I'd been a kid. As far as I know, it didn't actually have a name. Just a big sign on the front that read 'eat' in all caps. Not sure where the name Pedro's came from. Shit, I hope we weren't being racist. Actually, I think that might've been the name of the owner. Anyway, the food was awesome, cheap, and it gave us an inconspicuous place to talk about conspicuous things.

Michael and I spoke well into the night about things I really didn't want to believe in.

Chapter Eleven
The One

The next day, I ignored my alarm, slept a little late, and went downstairs after a lazy breakfast of a microwaved egg burrito. It's a pity the old alchemists didn't have microwaves. They spent so long trying to turn lead into gold, who know it would be this easy to turn bread into stone? Gotta eat it fast.

Never had being in my office felt so good. I knew this office. I knew my job, too. Both of them represented things quite normal, quite real. I liked normal and real.

This other stuff was... too crazy. Part of me still felt halfway certain I had dreamed the last two days. In fact, I'd been hesitant to test my newfound skills all morning. For now, mentally filing away the past few days as a dream afforded me a break I sorely needed. A rational explanation that made sense of it all.

So, I got back to work. Crystal Bradbury showed up a little after eleven, wanting an update on the case. Seeing her made me happy. She walked in on me making coffee at the little bar sink in the corner of my office. While it brewed, I headed back to my desk and sat across from her.

She looked... well, beautiful. If I hadn't noticed it before, I sure did today. If possible, her second impression was even more stunning. Quite frankly, I had been in a dating slump since Sheriff Justine Waters. More precisely, I hadn't wanted to date. I still didn't, not really. I enjoyed being alone. I enjoyed my quiet moments. In the past, my relationships had proven to be more troublesome than they were worth. In truth, I felt pretty certain I'd never been in full-blown love, even though I had said the words on occasion. That was okay. I loved my quiet life, instead. My simple life. I loved my books and TV shows, and my long walks. I even loved my job. Stakeouts were a great way to relax and quiet the mind.

Or maybe I merely kidded myself.

Perhaps I really did want a relationship and I just hadn't found 'The One,' as Ron always said. Could be I'd been terrified of finding my 'one' since that meant I could also lose her—as Ron had.

It surprised me to discover my heart beating a little faster than normal while I looked at Crystal. Geez, what was up with that? I hadn't felt quite this way the first time I met her, so why now? Sure, I had admired her beauty... but what's the deal with my pounding heart and shortness of breath?

I hadn't a clue, but something came over me. She literally took my breath away in her knee-ripped black jeans and faded, tight black T-shirt with Victoria's Secret spelled out in rhinestones across her chest. No bra, no makeup, no nail polish. Her hair was up in a casual ponytail, a messy one, even. She hadn't dolled herself up one bit and, yet, I had difficulty focusing.

To be completely honest with myself, I might have developed a goofy, school-boy crush on Crystal Bradbury. Like, right now. In that exact moment.

Lord help me, but the word *smitten* rolled across my mind.

"How are you holding up?" I asked, surprised I only stumbled slightly over my words. Schoolboy crush indeed.

"I'm holding up... I guess about as well as anyone can be after what happened. Have you learned anything yet about Dana's death?"

While I contemplated how, exactly, to answer her question, the coffee maker quit percolating, thus buying me a little time. I remembered how she liked her coffee the last time and, without asking her if she wanted a cup, made her one and brought it over.

"Two sugars and cream," I said.

"You remembered," she said, both eyebrows up.

"Here at Long Investigations, customer service is our top priority."

She smiled and sipped her coffee, making a face as if she enjoyed it. I enjoyed that she seemed to enjoy it.

Settle down, partner, I thought.

"About your sister," I said, still not sure of the direction I should take.

"You've discovered something." She set her coffee down and leaned forward. I had her full, unwavering, and perfect attention.

Lord help me.

Of course, by admitting exactly *what* I had discovered—that her sister had likely been killed by a vampire—I would also be admitting that the events of the past few days were not part of one long, drug-filled (even though I don't take drugs) hallucinogenic dream. No, I hadn't quite abandoned enough sanity to be willing to admit that yet. And definitely not to her. I needed to believe it all myself first. But how could I look this woman in her lovely, hypnotic eyes and lie to her?

I considered my options, then decided to pass the buck. "You're right, the police didn't investigate very deep into the attack. They saw—or wanted to see—'animal attack' and stopped the investigation right there."

"It was no animal, Mr. Long."

"I believe you," I said.

"Dana and Luke were being followed. Hunted. And not by an animal."

A chill swept over me as I recalled the autopsy photos. I prayed Crystal hadn't seen them. No sibling should have to see their sister's throat torn out. My God, the savagery. Had the bastard who'd shown up at my office done that? Sweet mama. If so, he was a killer through and through. And what would he have done to me had I gone down there to answer the door?

Well, he would have killed me, perhaps in a similar manner.

So why didn't I worry about being in my office now? Well, for one, it was late morning with a lot of sunlight out. And two... well, I wasn't so helpless now, was I?

No, very much not.

Dreaming, I thought. Not real. Refuse to believe. Head in sand.

Except here sat a woman—and not just any woman, but one causing a bio-physical reaction within me—openly crying angry tears, confused and needing answers. Answers I might actually have.

Time to take my head out of the sand.

Time to help.

Time to do my damn job.

Crystal waited expectantly for my answer with tears pooling upon her high cheekbones.

I opened my palm and summoned a small wind. A zephyr, I believe they called it.

It appeared instantly, ruffling her hair and the papers along my desk, small enough not to cause any alarm, although she shivered and rubbed her bare arms.

It's official, I thought, sighing. I'm a freak. She looked around, no doubt in search of the air vent responsible, then gave me the most curious of looks. I had a feeling she realized exactly what I'd done.

Way faster than Ron, too.

I took in some air, and reluctantly leveled my stare at her. "Do you believe in vampires, Miss Bradbury?"

Chapter Twelve
Matters Seldom Discussed

She blinked.

Since I'd never posed the vampire question to anyone, I wasn't sure what reaction I expected. The one she gave me would have been far, far down on the list.

Instead of laughing it off, or demanding I return her money for wasting her time—or being insane— she simply sat back, crossed her legs and folded her hands over her exposed knees. "Why do you ask, Mr. Long?"

To say her question and demeanor caught me off guard would be an understatement. I opened my mouth to speak, only to discover that I hadn't a clue what to say.

Crystal tilted her head. "Mr. Long?"

"You don't seem surprised by the question."

She shrugged, although the rest of her remained perfectly still. "The rumors of vampires around here are nothing new."

"Maybe," I said, knowing she was right, of course. "But your reaction is a first for me."

"Whatever do you mean?"

"You took my question in stride," I said. "Almost as if you had, well, expected it."

"Or perhaps I'm still too stunned to give you a proper response."

I shrugged. "Are you?"

She leaned forward. "Let's cut the crap, Mr. Detective. What do you know?"

"The town has a vampire problem, or so I'm told."

"Told by whom?"

By a blogger named Michael, I could have said, but didn't. "My sources... one of which happens to be my camera. You don't seem surprised."

"Maybe because I'm not, detective."

"If you knew it was a vampire who killed Dana and her husband, then why did you hire me?"

"Because I most certainly didn't *know*. Honestly, I don't understand much about vampires."

"But you know enough not to laugh off my original question."

She took in a lot of air. Some of my puppy love had faded, but as she inhaled again and her lungs expanded and her chest lifted, I might have swallowed. Hard. And I might have wet my lips a little, too.

After a long pause, she nodded. "I'm aware of the town's vampire problem. And the recent 'animal attacks' seem to confirm that the vampires are back, but I wouldn't know for sure. I'm not exactly in the loop anymore."

"Anymore?"

"I've said far too much, Mr. Long."

"On the contrary, you haven't said nearly enough. Dana and Luke, unless I'm wrong, were killed by a vampire. At least, that's what the evidence suggests."

"What kind of evidence?"

I told her about the too-small-for-a-cougar bite marks on the neck, the tree branch covered in blood that had been up far too high for any cat to carry its prey.

"What are you suggesting? That a vampire dragged my sister up the tree and fed on her from up there?"

"I'm not sure what I'm suggesting," I said, "but it's damn strange nonetheless."

"How did you come across this tree branch, if I might ask?"

"The tree branch had broken free." I looked away. "Probably in a windstorm."

"And you happened to arrive to witness this branch falling free?"

"I did. It fell at my feet."

"How fortuitous."

"My best guess is that the branch had been compromised by the combined weight."

"Is that your very best guess, Mr. Long?"

I swallowed at her penetrating look. Geez, did she know about me? Duh, I just demonstrated the wind for her. Of course she knew about me. I recovered and put on my most confident expression. "Yes, of course. What are you suggesting?"

"I'm suggesting nothing. All I know is that Dana is dead and the man I hired to find her just stumbled upon some very unlikely evidence."

I raised my hands. "Sometimes an investigator gets lucky."

"Fine. If it was a vampire, then where does that get us?"

"I don't know," I said. "But you still have some explaining to do. How do you know about the vampires here in Shadow Pines? And why did you say 'I said too much'?"

Crystal gave me another penetrating look. Then she nodded and stood. "Good questions, surely. But ones that I am not at liberty to discuss. Thank you for the coffee. I'll be back in a few days for another update."

She paused with one foot out the door. "Please be careful out there, detective."

Her voice carried real concern, but I couldn't come up with a response before she gave me a sad smile and left.

Chapter Thirteen
Of Life and Death

"You're not my first elemental, Max."

That's how Michael had begun our discussion on vampires last night. After we'd left Pedro's and torched the shack, we'd been sitting in a clearing with the waxing moon high overhead. Apparently, I wasn't the first to seek him out, nor would I be the last. Because he was in the know, he had been given sensitive information. In particular, information about the undead among us. I found myself believing him, trusting my gut about the guy.

Much of what I assumed about vampires was true, though a surprising amount of stuff I thought would be true wound up being false. Like crosses— or holy symbols in general. Michael didn't want to get into a long, belabored discussion of theology and told me that if any sort of god or higher power existed, vampires as well as other supernatural beings had to be part of that creation. One could not, for example, use a crucifix to ward off an angry bear. Some people regarded vampires as minions of Satan, but as Michael said, people of antiquity often blamed everything they didn't like or didn't understand on the Devil.

Aside from whether or not God had any opinion on vampires, Nature sure did. Michael told me that the undead—and slipped in a comment like 'of any type, not just vampires' without explaining—were basically 'anti-nature.' Everything had its opposite. That old adage about mountains not being mountains without flat ground and valleys to compare them to applied here. Also, vampires tended to be more powerful than humans due to numbers.

The way Michael described it... the Earth had a finite amount of life force, and an equal—but opposite—dark energy. Said life force was spread out among everything from microbes to plants to animals to humans. Same applied with the dark energy and vampires (or undead in general), only they existed in vastly inferior numbers, resulting in the opposite energy not being spread as thin. Since each vampire had more dark energy than a human had light energy, it made them more powerful. Kind of like they're the guys who drank ten cups of espresso each morning compared to a normal person's one.

Anyway, something was going on here in Shadow Pines that threw off that balance, hence

Nature giving me an extra helping of mojo. So, back to vampires. Sunlight, much to my surprise, did not destroy them. It did, however, seriously dampen their supernatural powers. Michael said it 'nerfed' them. Fire, however, worked wonders. He didn't fully understand the why of it, but the more powerful (or more evil) a vampire was, the more easily they caught fire. A sick bastard like the one who killed Dana would probably burn like a kerosene-soaked rag. Bullets, swords, and so on didn't do anything they couldn't recover from with the exception of wooden bullets.

Naturally, I laughed at the idea, but he showed me a YouTube video. Apparently, wooden bullets *could* work, but as 12-gauge shotgun slugs. The projectiles didn't have much stopping power in the real world, but since wood had such a devastating effect on vampires, the slugs basically behaved like a normal lead slug on a human. That is... death.

Anyway, a wooden stake in the heart would destroy them up to a certain age. On vampires much more than a century old, a stake only paralyzed them. Beheading could also kill them regardless of age. Garlic didn't do anything, and I already knew about the no reflection in mirrors thing and not showing up on video or cameras. However, that deal with having to invite them in was true. That threw me for a loop trying to figure out how the universe knew who could invite someone in... and did it apply only to a 'home,' or would offices be protected too? What would stop a vampire from dragging a pet human around, tossing them through a door and having their pet invite them in?

Thankfully, vampires did not have to kill to feed. The smarter ones who wished to avoid detection as much as possible would leave their victim alive but make them forget the feeding. With each bite, a person became more and more like a vampire. Someone who suffered three attacks too close together from the same vampire would turn. And it took something like four months for the negative energy of a bite to dissipate and reset the proverbial counter.

Among my many questions, I had asked how I would recognize a vampire... other than their lack of hands on my security camera, of course. His answer had been... interesting to say the least.

"You will sense them, Max. They won't be able to hide from you. If you are like the other elementals, then you will be fully equipped to sniff out the undead among you."

A few more questions later, I had pinpointed his meaning: the undead gave off a scent... and not a pleasant one. It didn't register with mortals, but it would register with me. We returned to town a little while before midnight. I invited him to stay with me, but he was too eager to get home and renew his research into the area.

***

That evening, late, I found myself back home

again; that is, upstairs in my apartment.

I stood at my kitchen window, looking down on the darkening street. Could Crystal be a vampire? After all, she had certainly known about them. Well, she didn't *feel* like a vampire. Nor did she smell anything but perfect. Yes, I had noted her floral perfume the instant she had opened the door, recognizing her without turning from my coffee making. Still, she had not seemed surprised about vamps. What the hell was up with that?

Michael briefly said something about their smell worsening the darker their souls had become. A 'reasonably nice' vampire might only smell like a dry tomb... a mild odor perhaps easily covered by floral perfume.

So was Crystal a nice vampire? Somehow, I doubted it.

I spent a while thinking about everything I'd learned and all the questions I'd come up with after he left. He'd come over to explain things—and to train me—but it felt like he'd left me even more confused. I hadn't even realized how much I didn't know until I started getting answers to the basic questions. Annoyed, confused, and with absolutely no idea what to do next, I flopped on the sofa, bare feet up on the coffee table, and cracked open a beer. To remind myself I hadn't dreamed everything, I let a small flame dance over my hand, weaving it around my fingers. Part of me still wanted to forget it all, but if the vampires knew who I was and wanted to kill me for it, I couldn't let my guard down. The memory of Crystal's scent distracted me, and I wound up thinking about her more than the problem at hand, hoping with every ounce of hope I could muster that she wasn't a vampire.

That would crush me.

A heavy knock rattled my apartment door.

I'll admit it. I jumped, nearly spilling my beer all over myself. I had the TV on despite not paying attention to it. I set the beer down, considered going for my gun—considered that a little extreme—and headed over to my front door. Admittedly, I didn't get a lot of visitors here, not a bad thing for a self-proclaimed hermit.

As I crossed the living room, the smell of death and decay hit me. The stink of rotting corpse. Shit, had something died in my walls again?

I paused, curious, sniffing the air. I'd once come across a dead body in the back of a Buick while working a case. The poor bastard had been bound and gagged... and rotting. Not pleasant, any of it. I'd had nightmares for months. Still do. Anyway, I would never forget that smell. It had a pungent sweetness to it that burned itself into the memory. The two smells, when combined, became absolutely revolting.

I got a hint of that in the air. Not quite as strong, certainly. But there it was. A hint of decay. A hint of death.

Yeah, a rat or maybe even a raccoon definitely died behind one of these old walls. I'd look into it later. When I reached the door—which always self-locks when shut—I looked out the peephole and recognized both men standing in the hallway, if, in fact, they were men: the handsome, dark-haired guy who had come knocking at my office door the other evening and the taller, long-faced guy with the Hollywood hair who had been at the cafe during my little demonstration with Ron.

Both appeared equally handsome, equally frightening. And seemed to stare at me in return right through the closed door.

This building used to be a hotel, but had been refurbished into a small apartment building about forty years ago. Beyond them was my neighbor's dull red door. I hoped Ruth stayed inside and kept her curiosity in check.

Perhaps more interesting, the scent of decay gathered strength, like the dead body sat right outside the door in the hall.

They're dead, said Michael's voice in my memory. *Always remember that. You are dealing with the walking dead.*

I swallowed and considered *not* opening the door. In fact, I started to back up.

The taller one said, "We can hear you breath-ing."

I paused, gathered myself, and mentally pre-pared myself for what was standing outside, if that was even possible.

After all, here be monsters.

I hesitated another heartbeat or two... then opened the door.

Chapter Fourteen
The Greasers

"Can I help you gentlemen?" I asked, pleasant enough, despite my heart beating somewhere up near my throat. Breathing, let alone swallowing, had become difficult.

"We're looking for a private dick," said the dark-haired bad boy. He emphasized the word *dick*.

The taller guy grinned, and asked, "Are you Max Long?"

Good cop, bad cop. Or maybe good vampire, bad vampire?

The smell of death had grown stronger with the door open, and it was obvious from whom or what the smell came from them. Indeed, the pair stank as if they'd just returned from robbing a grave. Maybe they had.

"You got him," I said, and tried not to gag.

"How can I help you?"

"We'd like to discuss some... business with you," said Hollywood. "May we come in?"

I recalled Michael's further instruction about never inviting a vampire in—or even someone who *might* be a vampire. Michael's exact words had been: "Get into the habit of not inviting *anyone* suspicious in."

But these two punks weren't the only cocky assholes around. I stepped back and motioned with a hand, indicating that they should come in. I hoped this gesture didn't qualify as an official invite. Must not have been, because neither of the men moved. My heart pounded in my ears. This was all so... unreal. Crazy, crazy, crazy.

"I can hear your heart beating," said the bad boy. He leaned a shoulder casually against the doorframe. "Nervous?"

"Should I be?"

"We're just here to talk," said the taller one, smiling warmly... or trying to. It looked creepy as hell. "Maybe you could invite us in?"

I motioned again. "No one's stopping you."

He smiled. I smiled. The bad boy didn't smile. Neither moved.

"So it's true. You two really *are* vampires," I said, stunned. I mean, just because I was dealing with weird shit, didn't entirely mean I was ready to accept the existence of vampires. Or even believe in them. But here they were... two of them, in the flesh... the very pale flesh.

"And why would you say a crazy thing like that?" asked the taller one.

"Because you can't step through my doorway unless I invite you in."

"Someone's been watching a little too much TV," said the shorter one.

They looked remarkably handsome. Either could've been movie stars. Both seemed in their twenties, the shorter one toward the older end. What their real ages were, I hadn't a clue.

The bad boy leveled a terrifying cold stare at me. "We should just kill him now."

"Ignore him," said the taller of the two to me, trying to smile warmly but failing. "My associate is a bit of a… well, psychopath."

"You say the sweetest things," replied the other.

I swallowed. Never had I seen such a lack of empathy. Mostly in the smaller one. The taller one wasn't too far off. Both were cold-blooded killers, of that much I felt certain.

"What are your names?" I asked. Truth was, I had asked around in town, but no one seemed to remember these two, which I found odd. "What's it hurt to tell me since, you know, you're gonna kill me and all?"

The psychopath appeared amused.

The tall one smiled broadly, showing a lot of teeth. I noted they were level teeth. As in, no pointy canines. "I'm Piper and this is Derek."

"So you guys partner up like cops?" I asked, trying to buy time. Other than my crash course in vampires last night, I knew next to nothing about the social structure of vampires. For all I knew, they often came in twos, although I doubted that. After all, Bad Boy had been alone when he came a-knockin' the other night. And Hollywood had been alone at the bar, watching my little air raid display.

Derek gave me a half smirk. "I like him. Too bad we have to kill him."

"He jokes," said Piper. "Ignore him."

Ignore him I did. "Do either of you have any information about the two people who were killed last week?"

"I wouldn't say I have much useful information." Derek crossed his arms over his chest, "but they were certainly delicious."

"You killed them?"

He shrugged. "It's kinda what I do."

Hearing his total disregard for human life sent a chill through me. His reaction made it ten times worse: The bastard *enjoyed* making me feel uncomfortable. A plague on the Earth indeed.

The tall guy pulled a gun, his movements so fast his hand blurred into a smear. "Well, now that the cat's out of the bag, maybe we should conclude our business. I expected there was a chance you would not let us in. Luckily, a bullet isn't beholden to the same irritating rules."

"Kill him, brother," said Derek. "Fuck the warning, and fuck him."

The taller vampire nodded and lifted the gun. Something flickered inside me and I reflexively raised my hands an instant before he pulled the trigger. White energy coalesced around the front end of the .45.

A muted *whump* came from the gun, loud, but nowhere near as loud as a gunshot ought to be. I stared for an instant in bewildered shock at a bullet trapped within a thick coating of ice that had frozen over the tip of the barrel. Out of nowhere, a sense of rage took me—a deep-seated aversion to these creatures' mere existence. The back end of the gun glowed brilliant orange, melting in Piper's hand. Turned out I didn't just create fire... but could make heat necessary for the fire. And I could do so quickly. Same with water. I didn't merely summon it via rainclouds, I could summon it from the air around me... and control the temperature of it as well. Neat tricks, both.

The tall vampire yelped and dropped the gun, his fingers on fire. While I hadn't made open flame by intent, vampires appeared rather prone to combustion. He waved his hand so fast it again blurred, and the fire went out.

A glint of metal flashed from Derek's belt. I thrust my left hand at him in a stopping motion as he went to throw a knife at me. More white energy streamed forth, coalescing into a large block of ice that froze the knife to his fingers. He grunted, struggling to hold up the weight of an icy sphere large enough to completely engulf the giant hunting knife. A normal human of his build wouldn't have been able to lift it one handed, but he managed it, albeit with difficulty.

He stared at it. I stared, too. Unreal. Wait, no… Awesome. But that exhilaration blossomed into fury once more. These two would no doubt go on killing innocent people, perhaps forevermore. Of course, I didn't want to burn down my house. The instant the intent formed in my mind, a light rain wet the floor in the hall, which I promptly froze into an ice sheet.

"What the hell..." said Derek, grabbing Piper, who still clutched his burned hand to his chest in pain.

I raised both arms, calling a gale that blasted them off their feet and sent them rocketing down the hall like a pair of limp bobsleds. They crashed into the radiator at the far end, six apartments away. Derek slammed into the wall hard enough that the ice ball broke away from his hand, the knife still stuck inside.

They scrambled upright and ran for the steps that led to the outside door. The ice on the floor evaporated to fog in response to my desire. I followed them, not entirely sure what to do next. By the time I rushed down the stairs to the sidewalk, they'd gone a fair way down the street, so I extended my right arm and summoned lightning. Two shafts of electricity connected my fingertips to their backs with an instantaneous crackle and a *boom* that flung them both off their feet and sent them sliding on their chests. Derek went face first into a tree while Piper struck a parked car. The pair bounced right back up, both smoking, and took off at a superhumanly fast sprint. I didn't quite trust my skill at the moment to chase them into a potential ambush, nor did I want to put on too much of a magic show. The last thing I needed was fame. The people of Shadow Pines would lose their damn minds if I kept doing magic out in the open.

Piper, with the burned hand, appeared the most freaked out by what I'd done. So much so, he kept looking back over his shoulder at me—and crashed into a tree.

I couldn't help but laugh at them.

That lightning bolt should have been enough to knock the crap out of them. The last time I'd called a bolt that big while training with Michael, it had split a dead tree in half.

I made my way back upstairs, still chuckling when I closed my door.

Those two vamps had murder in their eyes. Had I been anyone less than what I was—an Elementalist apparently—I would be dead, shot through the heart... or worse if I had actually invited them in.

My case took a turn for the strange, but at least I'd found the ones responsible for the deaths. Both of them were killers, no *monsters*.

They enjoyed killing.

Chapter Fifteen
Killers

The vampires rattled me.

I did some research using some websites not available to the general public. In order to access them, one needed to sign up and pay a subscription fee as well as send proof of access, like my PI license, or a valid law-enforcement ID. As far as I could tell, no record existed of men named Derek and Piper being born anywhere in this area. Of course, their names had to be false, but they'd been using them for a while at least. I found a man named Piper Burroughs registered as the owner of a handful of cars, and he owned an old boarding house a little ways outside of town. I knew of the place, but had never gone there. It sat mostly hidden behind a thick wall of shrubs and trees, and of course it had been the subject of countless scary stories.

I sat back and rubbed my face. So that's where the town's vampires lived. Well, at least two of them. Michael had made it clear that nature wouldn't have summoned an elemental unless there was a real problem afoot. More than likely, I'd have to deal with more than only those two vamps, and possibly other creatures, like werewolves. If I saw an actual werewolf running in the woods... yeah, I think I would freak. Please let those be fake. Vampires I can handle. I had seen the pretty boy face of vampires. I could handle the vampires, I think. I'd certainly handled them well enough tonight, but I expected them to regroup and come out swinging. Hopefully, I would be ready for them.

I went further back in time, a deep dive into the database and resources. Piper had purchased the home... wow, twenty years ago. And neither one of them looked much older than their mid-twenties.

"They really are vampires," I whispered. "Freakin' a."

I went back further, but found no additional evidence of them. I suspected these two likely changed their names often, as well as changed towns. After twenty years here, they were likely getting ready to move on again. That could explain the recent surge of attacks. If they're planning to leave the area, why restrain themselves? Go crazy for a while, have fun, then vanish. I'd seen them often throughout the years, but never paid much attention to how little their appearance had changed. Funny how the brain worked. I suspected they might somehow change the way they looked, too, when they decided to reinvent themselves and relocate. Anything to keep people off balance. And if someone suspected anything, or asked them about their anti-aging regime, that someone probably ended up dead... or missing. I was willing to bet that huge boarding house of theirs contained more than a few skeletons in its closets, and not metaphorical ones. That place likely held the answers to the many deaths and missing persons cases that plagued this town.

I drummed my fingers for a while, lost in thought, and finally shut off my computer. With any luck, I wouldn't suffer a nocturnal visit from an uninvited vampire. I should be able to get a decent night's sleep.

Should being the operative word...

***

The next day, I returned to the woods, standing not too far away from where Dana Bradbury-Hayden and her husband had been killed.

I had seen the face of the killer, and he'd shown no remorse. No humanity. If anything, he had the look of a hunter proud of a kill. I told myself they merely looked like humans. Both were killers through and through, especially the smaller one, Derek. Piper, I still had a few doubts about. Then again, he had pulled the gun on me; worse, he had pulled the trigger. Yup, he'd had every intention of killing me. Still, I didn't get a psychopath vibe from him. Trying to shoot me had been self-preservation. Still, I suspected taking human life didn't exactly keep him up at night—or keep him up during the day... whatever.

No doubt they'd killed many people throughout the years, and I'd wound up on their hit list.

Well, I wasn't just anyone now, was I?

Nature had seen to that. Nature had given me an edge.

Then again, Nature had also put a big target on my back, too.

"Thanks, Nature," I said and threw a rock over the cliff into the churning pool of water far below.

Those two were... evil. I could feel it wafting off them like a stink so bad it made the air blurry. Literally, in fact. I definitely smelled it. And yet, I had seen them associating with others in town. In particular, the college girls. I hoped to God they weren't dating them.

Creeps.

Had they compelled their girlfriends? Could vampires love? From what I had seen standing outside my apartment... the answer was a resounding no. Then again, where had that fury that overwhelmed me come from? Yes, my life had been threatened—casually and wantonly—but shouldn't I have been more worried than angry? In truth, I didn't scare easily... and I might've possessed the sort of courage that transcended simple bravery and went into the realm of foolishness. A good trait for a PI. Timid people didn't do well in this job. I get threatened often. Maybe not to my face, and maybe not so blatantly with a gun, but that wasn't my first death threat. So, what had triggered my reaction? Hard to say, but in that moment, I felt a true hatred for these things. I wanted to do much worse than zap their asses with lightning... I wanted to strangle the life out of them... except, of course, they were immortal. Guess I'll need to use fire.

And I'm not a killer, dammit. No matter how much I wanted to do away with those two cocky bastards. But, I had to keep telling myself that I dealt with the undead. They only looked like people. Any humanity they may once have had died an unknown time ago when whatever fiend who turned them did it. Or maybe they'd been psychos in life. I had no idea if simply becoming a vampire could transform a normal person into a heartless killer or if it only worsened what already existed.

My fury had to be part of the change that had come over me. Michael warned me about it, and I saw the evidence of it. If a death threat alone wouldn't get me to wage a private war against these two immortal greasers, then my irrational hatred for them would. That, and thinking about the people they've murdered—and would kill in the future. The best explanation I could come up with involved something of a 'matter/antimatter' reaction between the Nature energy inside me and the dark energy that comprised vampires.

But some part of hunting them down and killing them in their coffins struck me as wrong. Assuming, of course, they actually slept in coffins. Michael hadn't said anything about it. Fair chance the coffin thing was pure Hollywood. It sounded too silly to be plausible. Then again, the 'can't come inside unless invited' sounded silly, and it proved true. Still, I had a suspicion they'd spare me the moral conundrum of having to decide if I wanted to destroy them. They would likely come gunning for me sooner or later.

Although Michael and I had trained the other night—and I suspected the full extent of my power was still unknown even to me—I felt I'd need weeks if not months of training to take on these two. Sure, I had gotten the upper hand on them last night, but they knew what I was capable of now and wouldn't make the mistake of casually strolling up to 'chat' again. I had shown my hand... and had given them a taste of my power. If they had any way to prepare themselves for our next meeting, I'm sure they'd be ready for it. Next time, they wouldn't walk up and knock on my door—they'd be jumping out at me from a dark alley.

"Did you see how fast he drew that gun?" I asked myself, staring down into the churning water. "Had he not been so chatty, I might not have had time to manipulate the elements."

That's how I explained what I did: I thought of myself as manipulating the elements. I didn't know how the hell I did so, but I did. My intent became a matter of fact. If I wanted something to happen, it happened within reason. Nature appeared to be listening to me and doing what I asked it to.

"You and nature are one, Max." Michael tried to convince me of that over and over. "There are even some who claim that you are the incarnation of nature itself. Its physical manifestation."

"No," I had said. "That's where you're wrong. I'm just me, as I had been for twenty-eight years."

Of course, Michael only shrugged and gave me that 'silly mortal' look. Although as far as I knew, he was not immortal. At least, I didn't think so.

What did I know of fighting bloodthirsty immortals? Not much, if anything. Only what Michael told me. Great, I'd trusted my destiny to a middle-aged blogger who looked like Jerry Seinfeld's neurotic friend. The only thing I knew for sure is that blood would spill.

To ensure it wasn't mine, I decided to come out here, in the quiet of the woods, and practice my connection with the elements more, trying every possible way I could think of to manipulate things. After all, creating the thunderbolts had occurred to me on a whim, and it had worked out perfectly. Well, not so much. The vampires kept on running. Now, I made it rain, hail, snow… I threw lightning from my hands, chucked fireballs, made sheets of flame form in the air, and even opened pits in the Earth the size of swimming pools by commanding the dirt and rock to move and flow like liquid. Hmm…

What else could I do?

As the day wore on, I continued practicing my form of strange Nature magic, knowing I faced a high likelihood of needing it soon.

Very soon.

Chapter Sixteen
The Families Have Skeletons

Crystal Bradbury and I sat in my truck.

I'd parked outside of town near the abandoned stone quarry a little past three in the afternoon. Below us, the ground yawned open in a massive pit something on the order of six stories deep. All the natural resources within robbed by man. Interestingly, I could almost feel the assault on the Earth, feel its life force being stolen, ripped away. Then again, I was an Elemental. Or, so I had been told.

For me, this didn't feel like another client meeting. For me, this felt like something a little more. Being around her triggered weird emotions deep in my gut that dredged up memories of being an awkward high school junior with a crush on a cheerleader. For Crystal Bradbury, not so much. I sincerely doubted she had any sort of feelings for me beyond 'this idiot is getting nowhere' or 'I'm wasting money.' Even hoping that she felt something similar for me as I felt about her was not only doubtful, but selfish on my part. After all, my life had just gone from mundane to insane.

How could I possibly inflict that life onto someone else?

And, for that matter, how un-freakin'-fair was it that I should meet a girl *now* who made my breath catch in my throat every time I saw her? I mean, I'd spent years and years alone, living peacefully and comfortably, seeking out a simple, if not boring, existence. That would have been an ideal time to meet my soulmate.

Soulmate, pal? Seriously?

Wishful thinking. Honestly, I wasn't even sure what soulmate meant anymore. I did know that the girl sitting next to me had captured my heart unlike any other in all my life.

My weird Elemental, fire-starting, rain-creating, wind-blowing heart.

I sighed as I looked out over the great pit, where miners had spent years removing gypsum and iron ore and God knew what else. The mine, long since depleted, had been abandoned for years and sat like a scar on the Earth, a few miles outside of town. Funny, I had never thought of it as a scar before. Truth be known, I had had no feelings about it.

But now I did. Go figure.

Crystal had parked her car, a newish little sporty thing, next to my truck. She had arrived with two iced coffees, which I thought considerate of her. We made some small talk, and I gushed like a smitten teen. I couldn't tell if she knew I gushed. Maybe she just thought I had a speech impediment. Maybe she noticed and chose not to react.

"So, now that you have me out here in the middle of nowhere, overlooking your bizarre idea of a scenic view..." Crystal sipped her iced coffee while watching me. "What did you want to talk about?"

"Vampires," I said.

She nodded and continued watching from over her plastic cup. "I figured as much."

"I met two of them last night. Figure they're pretty old since they both dress like they haven't quite gotten over the Fifties."

"Derek and Piper, I assume."

I glanced at her. "You assume correctly. How do you know about them?"

"You could say my family has a long history with them. Why do you bring them up?"

"Well, for one, because they are vampires."

"Mr. Long, in this town, that doesn't mean much."

"What do you know of this town?" I asked.

"Nuh-uh, Mr. Detective Man. You tell me why you brought up those two guys first, and then I'll tell you what I know. Maybe."

I sipped my coffee, squinting at the strong sun warming my face. Michael said vampires could go out in the daytime, the sun only robbed them of the majority of their power. Still, creatures like that hated being weak and vulnerable, so they generally tried to avoid daylight—especially when they knew of a dangerous enemy nearby. I had to admit, I suspected Crystal might have been a vampire as well, but she didn't give off any pungent hint of death. In fact, she still smelled good. Real damn good. With no perfume on at all, her fragrance contained hints of toothpaste, soap, and the sun-kissed skin of a girl with silky platinum blonde hair who liked the outdoors, probably as much as I did.

She's no vampire. She's too...clean.

I considered her proposal, then nodded. "Okay, then. I'll tell you what I know, if you tell me what you know."

"You might have yourself a deal there, partner." She flashed a coy smile.

"Derek all but admitted to killing them."

Crystal had been about to drink from her straw when she paused. "He said that?"

"Actually, yes. Worse, he seemed proud of it."

"He's always been a dick."

"You seem to know him," I said.

"I know *of* him through whisperings from my family. Remember, Mr. Long. I don't live in town, and for the most part, I have been shunned. I am not privy to all their secrets."

"But you know about the vampires?"

"All the Founding Families are aware of the vampire presence in the area, Mr. Long. Especially the Bradburys, the Farringtons, the Blackwoods, and the Wakefields."

I knew of the Founding Families, of course. You couldn't go anywhere in this town without hearing something about them, or celebrating something about them. If ever a town existed that idolized its forefathers and foremothers, it would be Shadow Pines. For this being America, the locals sure liked to treat certain families like royalty. After everything I'd recently learned, the way everyone acted around them started to make sense—and for more reasons than those nine families having eighty percent of the wealth around here.

"Privy in what way?" I asked.

"Some of the Founding Families have made it their life's mission to control the vampire problem... and some of them work *with* them."

"No kidding."

"I'm not kidding."

"During the day?"

She nodded. "Whenever they have to. Depends on what is asked of them. The arrangements, as far as I know, tend to be mutually beneficial between the families and the vampires. Though, some of the families have made their name by opposing the vampires whenever possible."

"Kind of ballsy of them to walk around in daylight."

Crystal gave me this stare that called me clueless. "Vampires are not destroyed by sunlight, Mr. Long. That's a bit of fiction that came about after the film *Nosferatu*. Have you ever read Bram

Stoker?"

"Umm. Can't say I have."

"Color me unsurprised. There's no mention of sunlight affecting them in that novel... and from what I've heard, the events that transpired within that book were based on actual events—though no one dared admit that part. Some of the vampires here in Shadow Pines occasionally work for the sheriff and other family members. They have proven to be helpful at times...."

For the sheriff? Did Justine know about the vampires? "While other times they kill wantonly," I said.

She nodded. "Yes."

"They have to be stopped."

"I agree." She set her jaw. "I don't much like vampires."

We had both nearly finished our iced coffees, though I nervously kept sucking on the straw. The sun crept inexorably toward the western horizon, shining even more in our faces. I relished the warmth, even as my mind raced. "They said something else, too."

Crystal looked at me. "Do tell."

"They said that it had come to their attention that I was much more than a private detective."

"Oh? And why would they say that? Do you have your own deep dark secret, Max?"

God, I loved the way she said my name, drawing it out like a caress. I focused my slightly scattered thoughts. I debated how much to tell her.

Really, really debated, then said, "I think so, yes."

And then I told her everything, I mean *every-thing*.

Except the part where I wanted to spend the rest of my life with her.

That, I kept to myself.

Chapter Seventeen
Dirty Little Secret

We sat there for a while in a long awkward silence.

Eventually, Crystal looked over at me. "Are you a religious man, Mr. Long?"

"Not overly. I mean, sure, I believe in God, but I couldn't tell ya the last time I went to church." Truth be told, I'd always felt more spiritually alive out here in the woods. Guess I understand why now. "And, that's a bit of a random question... you wondering if I've got a bunch of crucifixes or something in the back to take on the vampires with?"

She giggled. "No. Those won't help. I'm asking if you're the sort of person who'd hear the word 'witch' and want to start screaming."

"You're a witch?"

"No." She batted her eyes at me and my heart

fluttered in response. "But people who hate witches aren't terribly fond of the sort of secret I have either. There's a reason my family sent me away and wants nothing to do with me. I'm a bit of an embarrassment to them."

I couldn't imagine what a girl like her could possibly do to be an 'embarrassment' to anyone. "What'd you do? Keep using the wrong fork for the salad course?"

Crystal emitted a clipped laugh. "No, Mr. Long. A minor breach of manners like that would hardly have been enough to be cast out. I have not shared my secret with many people. However, I also haven't met anyone else who can make the wind and rain obey or fire appear from thin air."

"Well, that makes two of us. To be honest, it's all kinda new for me."

She smiled. "Well, you've also seen vampires and you're not losing your mind."

"Heh. I've been told I don't rattle easy. And, well, I'm stubborn. Or 'pig headed' as my ex-girlfriend would say."

"The sheriff." She glanced off out the side window. "That woman is a tool."

"She's not *that* bad."

Crystal rolled her eyes. "No, Mr. Long. I mean a literal tool. She is under the control of vampires, at least she has been for the past year or two. Specifically, those aligned with the Farrington family. I'm sure you noticed how convinced she was that nothing more unusual than an animal attack caused Dana and Luke's death?"

"She's always been like that. Gets an idea in her head and good damn luck changing her mind, even with evidence."

"Well, she's not important now. The law is of no help in dealing with vampires. In a place like Shadow Pines, the important individuals within the local government are controlled and the others won't believe the truth. We can't go to the FBI for the same reason."

I tapped my fingers at the wheel. "They'd think we're crazy. And if I tried to prove it to them"—I summoned a small fire in my palm—"I'd either be shot, sent to a lab, or handed over to the CIA to do who-knows-what."

"Yes. It's why I tell so few people about my dirty little secret."

"What could you possibly have done that made your family consider you an embarrassment?"

"It's not anything *I* did, rather what my mother did." Crystal gradually turned toward me, making eye contact. "You see, I'm not exactly normal."

"No one who lives in Shady Pines is nor—"

Her eyes started glowing red-orange. Curved horns grew out from her temples, twisting back like a cute little ram. I have no idea how on God's green Earth she managed to do so, but... she became even more beautiful. The effect lasted only a moment before she once again appeared normal, which is to say, merely breathtaking.

"Okay. I stand corrected. That's unusual even

for this town."

My more or less blasé reaction seemed to reassure her enough to add sincerity to her smile. "Thoughts?"

"You have horns," I said.

"I do." She bit her lip, pouring on the demure smile. "I have a few other surprises, too."

"Are they invisible?"

Crystal took my hand and brushed it across her temple where the horn had been. Her hair had the softness of a rabbit's fur, and I felt nothing there that shouldn't be. "They go... somewhere else. I suppose it's similar to how the werewolves shapeshift. But I'm not a lycanthrope. I'm what's called a succubus, Max."

I blinked. "A succu-what?"

"Succubus. Or at least half of one. Or maybe three-quarters. I don't understand exactly how that works. And as far as I know, I'm not a demon."

"If demons could make themselves look as... angelic as you, that would be..."

"You're too kind." She blushed. "I believe we're more fey than demon, though depending on who you ask... fey and demons aren't terribly far removed from each other."

I mulled that for a little while. My knowledge of succubi came entirely from movies and a handful of books I'd read years ago, which is to say almost nothing and probably all bullshit. However, those sources all had the recurring theme of sex. "Did your father or mother walk in on something... awkward?"

She laughed. "No. Father knew exactly what I was the whole time. Mother had been charmed by an incubus. Of course, my human father didn't hold it against her since she'd been powerless to resist and unable to control herself. Once I came of a certain age and my... presence became too distracting for anyone who visited the house, I was sent away. To those outside the family, I'm the product of an affair that my father forgave my mother for."

That's only a little uncomfortable to think about. The former mayor sending his 'daughter' away because guests felt a strong attraction to her. From the moment I first laid eyes on her, she'd stirred feelings in me I thought I'd never have for a woman again. Oddly enough, not what I would've guessed from a succubus, like overwhelming lust. Her presence called to me on a deeper level, a 'this is the woman I want to grow old with' sort of level.

It occurred to me at that moment that perhaps a real succubus would trigger whatever appealed to a man's inner self most. And after seeing how well things worked out with Justine (sarcasm), simple lust evidently wasn't enough for me to carry on anything long term. Who could've guessed? And, sure... I thought Justine was a fascinating, intelligent, capable woman. We simply didn't click. That made me also wonder if how I saw Crystal as an innocent-faced ingénue too delicate for the harshness of the world, a girl in need of protection... did that come from her power trying to trick me into fulfilling some sort of 'protector' role?

"How much of your appearance is what I want to see compared to what is?"

Crystal regarded me for a long moment. "That's incredibly sweet of you, but I am neither as innocent as I appear nor as helpless. This is, how-ever, how I look to everyone. The"—she held up a hand, waving her fingers—"delicateness is from the fey side of the family."

Well, there's that. "Okay." I blink. "Are you reading my mind or assuming what I thought?"

"Yes." She fluttered her eyes at me.

I sat there a moment, then nodded, not quite sure what to think.

"I'm not evil, Max. I need you to understand that. I do like to have fun, be wild, indulge in certain vices… I've never had the patience for an overabundance of rules or being *proper*, which only made my family want me around less. They may be pricks, but I still love them—except for Grand-mother… she's been a real bitch to me. Dana was the only one who never acted like I'd become a pariah. We were quite a bit closer than half-sisters ought to have been."

Hmm. I rubbed my chin, realizing I needed to shave soon. The dead sister hadn't shunned her like the rest of the family. Perhaps the others objected to this? "Do you think your relationship with Dana is the reason she'd been targeted? I'm getting the feel-ing the attack wasn't as random as it appeared."

She fidgeted at her shirt where it draped in her

lap, her expression at an unreadable place between deep thought, an imminent explosion of tears, and wanting to tear someone's face off. Hopefully, not mine. After a few minutes, she looked up. "I suppose it is possible they targeted her, but I don't think her simply treating me like a sister she'd grown up with and not an outcast would've been enough to have her killed."

"Do you think she might've seen something that night in the woods they didn't want her revealing?"

"They?"

I shrugged. "A targeted murder is ordered by someone. Whoever did it is the *they*. Your family, another family, an as-yet-unknown vampire, perhaps even Piper sent his buddy to attack them... who knows?"

"Well, Dana did say something unusual on the call that I hadn't told anyone about. 'Crimony biscuits.'"

"Is that some odd British dessert?"

She managed a weak smile. "No, it's from a series of books we read as children. It's about this girl and her friend who basically run around solving mysteries. And of course, they run into stuff like mummies and monsters and evil wizards. More often than not, each story has a character in it that seems nice and friendly but turns out to be working for the bad guys—or *is* the bad guy. Whenever Drusilla, the main girl, realizes this or sees something dangerous, she always says 'crimony biscuits.'"

"I'm guessing she says that because they can't

put 'aww fuck' in a kids' book."

That got a laugh out of her. "Yeah, probably."

"But, Dana never used that phrase in real conversation. I'm sure she blurted it as a clue of some kind. Either she'd seen something extremely strange and dangerous, or... someone I trust is really a threat."

"But she didn't want to say it outright?"

"Maybe."

"Hmm... perhaps she *did* see something that someone wanted to keep quiet. Question is, what? And who sent Derek after her?"

"I'm sure Piper wasn't far behind. Two peas in a pod. Both equally psychotic in their own way. Don't let Piper's charm fool you. He makes Ted Bundy look like a saint."

I nodded. That, I could believe. "Perhaps they were the ones who made the decision to kill her?"

"I can't answer that. But I do think you need to put Piper and Derek out of this town's misery. My misery, too."

"Oh?" I sent a cocky half smile in her direction. "Why would a succubus need plain ol' me to deal with her vampire problem?"

She poked me. "You're far from 'plain old.' And I'm not equipped to deal with vampires. I can outrun them. I'm more or less as fast as they are..." My empty coffee cup appeared to teleport from the dashboard in front of me to her hand. Only the breeze across my face gave away that she'd grabbed it... yeah, that was an awesome display of speed.

"But, everything I might do to them—magically speaking, if you want to call it that—they'll recover from. So, I'm stuck using the same kinds of weapons anyone else would. Wooden stakes, fire —"

"Wooden bullets might work, too."

Crystal blinked. "Say again?"

"Wooden bullets, and they're not as crazy as you might think."

"Wouldn't they... I dunno... shatter or something?"

"Depends. I did a little looking on the internet. You get a hard enough type of wood and make a big enough bullet, say a 12 gauge shotgun slug, they can be fired. Range is crap, and they don't have too much stopping power on a normal human... but supposedly they could kill vampires."

She shrugged. "Wood is wood, I guess. As long as it penetrates the heart. Yet another example of the natural world foiling the unnatural. Who would think something as simple as wood could take down something as vile as a vampire?"

I shrugged. "I don't write the rules, but makes a kind of sense to me."

"Of course it would to you. You're like, nature personified."

"Maybe, maybe not. But if something were to stop the beating of an undead heart, exposure to something once deeply connected to the earth mother should do the trick."

"But the wood is dead, too."

"But it was once connected to the earth itself, and undoubtedly infused with light energy."

"So, would a thorn from a rose bush kill a vamp, then?"

"Doubtful, but it would do serious harm. No, I'm sensing trees are essential. Their sheer size and deep roots go far in retaining the earth energy to put one of those suckers down."

She giggled at 'suckers,' then added, "You're forgetting that normal people can't simply run around town with a shotgun without being arrested. Or make wooden bullets for that matter. Stakes might still be the best option... but you are far better equipped to deal with them. And no, I didn't know that about you at all when I hired you."

Again, I rubbed my chin in thought. "You do bring up a good point in that those two should probably be dealt with in a fairly permanent manner. Can't help but feel a bit strange about it though. It's never been in me to just kill someone like that."

"For one thing, they're not 'someones.' They're 'somethings.' Vampires are already dead. You wouldn't be killing anything, just making an already-dead corpse stop walking around. For another thing, they want to kill you and won't stop until they do."

"And... if I do anything other than put them down, I'll spend the rest of my life looking over my damn shoulder for the next ambush."

"That too." She held up a finger, wide-eyed. "Just remember they're killers, Max. How many innocent lives have they taken besides Dana's and Luke's? How many more innocent lives will they take in the future?"

"Fine." I squeezed both hands on the steering wheel, gripping it tight to bleed off angst at what felt like making myself into the judge, jury, and executioner. The girl did have a good point though. Piper and Derek had already died, *were* dangerous killers, and did want my ass on a morgue slab on the sooner side of later. "What kind of fallout do you think will happen if I get rid of these two?"

She pursed her lips in thought. "That would mostly depend on which family they're working for, assuming one is pulling their strings. If they did attack Dana at random, there won't be any repercussions at all short of whatever vampire friends they may have wanting to settle the score. But, it isn't as though the others would magically know what happened to Derek and Piper—not to mention, those two don't seem the type to make friends."

I chuckled. "No shit. Are all vampires as psycho as they are?"

Crystal glanced over at me with an apologetic expression. "I don't know. Father started sending me to school in Ironside when I was a junior. When I turned eighteen, they kicked me out and I had to live there, too. For whatever reason, the vampires don't go to Ironside too often. As a younger girl, I occasionally saw one in the house, but kept my distance. They didn't pay much attention to me either, likely because Fey blood is toxic to them."

"That's handy. How toxic are we talking here? Drop dead from a drop or 'sketchy Mexican restaurant' toxic?"

She furrowed her eyebrows at me for a second, then evidently decided to ignore my stupid joke. "If one were to bite me, their fangs would most likely disintegrate before they could pull them out."

"Ouch. So your blood is basically like acid to them."

"So I have been told. I've not seen proof of it." She pointed at me. "And don't get any funny ideas about... about making succubus hand grenades."

I raised my hands as if in surrender. "Not even going there. You might not *be* innocent, but you look it. Wouldn't dream of doing anything that would get you hurt, least of all using you or your blood as a weapon."

"Aww." She batted her eyelashes at me. "You are so cute."

"Right... so, how do we do this?"

She gestured at the ignition. "Why not find them and simply light them on fire."

"That sounds too simple."

"Lighting things on fire is a simple way to solve problems. Sometimes, the barbarian approach is the best."

Merely thinking about the way Derek grinned when confessing that he'd murdered Dana set off a wave of anger inside me, which I'm sure came from the elemental power I'd been given. Perhaps I'd become a 'creature' as well, diametrically opposed to vampires. Nature was full of powerful opposing forces: light and dark, life and death, efficiency and government.

The part of my psyche that recoiled at the idea of walking up and simply ending someone had been chewing on the facts of this case. Yeah, those two hadn't been human in a long time. They sure as hell *smelled* like dead bodies. They'd murdered Dana and her husband as casually as an out-of-town hiker tossing an apple core into the forest. They'd surely murder again. And again.

So, yeah. I had to put a stop to that. Suppose that's what Michael meant when he told me the universe gave me this power for a reason. And, I even had an idea of where to look.

That old boarding house. I'd lay fair odds I'd find them there.

"Got an idea where to look."

"The old boarding house?" she asked.

"You know about it?"

"I've had my suspicions. Let's go."

I nearly told her to stay here or go home, but I saw the resolve in her eye. It was, after all, her half sister and brother-in-law who'd been murdered. Plus, I suspected she could take care of herself, when push came to shove. "Do you want to follow me or move your car somewhere?"

"It's okay. I can get back to it if I have to."

I glanced over at her. "Uber?"

She giggled. "Not quite. Horns aren't my only extra body parts." She made a wing-flapping gesture. "But, I'd rather you gave me a ride back."

"Sure." I started the engine. "Givin' a pretty girl a ride is the least I can do."

And, wait. Did she just imply she could... fly?

She did. My God, she did.

Chapter Eighteen
Shadow Pines Manor

It might not have been the best time to pursue a confrontation with vampires, being only a few hours before sunset.

Then again, no time like the present, right? That, and sitting around not doing something about them could get more people killed. That word 'people' bounced around in my head for the entire fifteen minutes or so it took me to drive from the quarry, across town, and to the old boarding house. Both the quarry and the vampires' lair sat in the outskirts of Shadow Pines, but not on the same side. Piper and Derek—or whatever their actual names had been—used to be people, but I couldn't dwell on that now. Whatever humanity they once possessed had disappeared a long time ago. For all I knew, they could have been born during the Great Depression as easily as the Civil War or hell, even the American Revolution.

Though, their 'greaser' fashion sense probably meant they'd died in the fifties. My operational knowledge of vampires remained limited, though I had heard that they tended to become more powerful with age. If such rumors had any truth to them, I damn sure hoped these two were only around sixty years as vampires and not hundreds.

Crystal kept quiet as we drove across town and headed onto one of the backwoods roads to the southwest.

The isolation of the remote country made me think back to how little fight the two had put up when they confronted me at home. Initially, I'd wondered if it had been due to my not inviting them in, but even after I'd pursued them outside, they kept running. It didn't seem likely that I'd frightened them senseless. Most ordinary people probably would have shit themselves and run from a guy conjuring ice and lightning from his hands. However, as far as I knew, even lightning wouldn't cause permanent harm to vampires. Sure it *could* light them on fire if I got lucky. Neither one of them knew I could conjure open flame yet. Okay, so I superheated the gun, but heating metal and making fire fly out of my hand isn't the same. The hot-hand on the gun was far subtler than throwing fireballs. Call me silly, but I hadn't wanted to risk burning down the building I live and work in.

I didn't want to delude myself into feeling like

this would be easy, as if I were an exterminator going after roaches. I'm sure these two wouldn't simply roll over and die like pests, especially not when I'm the one invading their home. Regardless of what made them run last time, I had a sneaking suspicion that wouldn't be the case today, and I couldn't allow myself to become overconfident.

Hell, I didn't even feel confident yet.

This elemental thing is too new for me, and part of me still waited to wake up.

A few minutes after we left downtown behind, I spotted an old wooden sign and pulled off onto an overgrown road—more of a pair of tire ruts in dirt with gravel between them than an actual road—that veered off into the woods. I stopped to gather my thoughts, staring at the sign I'd seen so many times before but never bothered to take a close look at. It had, at one time, been plain white with black lettering, but five decades of sitting out in the forest with no maintenance resulted in varying shades of brown and fungus.

Shadow Pines Manor
Boarding House
Men or Women welcome
Rooms by the month - $150
Rooms by the week - $40

"The name of that place makes it sound like an old folks' home," I muttered.

Crystal glanced at me with an expression that

said she found my observation lame, but also faintly endearing. "Technically, it is housing the elderly. The *very* elderly... though they're not people anymore."

"We've got maybe two hours of daylight left."

"I doubt it will matter." She swiped at her hair, pulling it off her face so she could see with *both* eyes.

"Wait... aren't they weaker or something in the day?"

"Yes, but they're not going to be outside, are they?" She gestured at the trail stretching off ahead of us. "They've been living in this place for years. It's rather likely all the windows are boarded up to keep it dark inside."

"Great." I eased off the brake and let the truck roll forward. "So they become weaker when exposed to the sunlight, not based on what time it is?"

"Precisely."

"Does that mean they never sleep? Geez, no wonder they're insane."

She chuckled. "I'm afraid I don't understand it exactly, but I do know they sometimes do something that looks like sleep. How often or for how long, I haven't a clue. But it isn't tied to sunrise or sunset."

"Maybe we should approach on foot so they don't hear the truck coming?"

"They'll hear us on foot, too. It's like trying to sneak up on a paranoid cat. You might as well drive the whole way. It will give them less time to prepare."

I nodded and accelerated a little, pushing the truck up to around twenty-five. "Just need to be careful I don't get us trapped in a burning house."

She glanced at me with a flat expression. "You can create fire out of nothing. Can you not send it back where you called it from?"

My brain got stuck. All the time I'd spent with Michael trying to learn how to work this elemental thing, not once had I even considered the notion of 'un-making' fire. Sure, I'd put it out with rain, but 'reverse-creating' the fire directly hadn't even occurred to me. I'd been too awestruck at being able to summon it... like a small boy who'd discovered matches for the first time. "Umm. Yeah, that makes sense, but I haven't tried it."

"Unless you are looking forward to a drawn-out fight and possibly death, I suggest you learn fast and use fire on them."

"What are you going to do?"

She shrugged. "Improvise, I suppose."

The long, winding driveway ended at a giant dirt parking lot overgrown with weeds and untamed grass. An enormous three-story house that had clearly seen better days sat on the left. To the right, a particularly dense forest came right up to the edge of the dirt. The second and third floors had balconies bordered by wrought-iron fencing well into the process of falling off. Every window had boards covering them, except for a handful of giant bay windows on the ground level, which had been blocked off from the inside by heavy curtains. Ivy crept up the walls, though the plants gave off a sense of sickness, no doubt objecting to the dark energy within. In fact, the entire property gave me the feeling of a necrotic lesion gradually spreading decay into the woods.

"Yeah… they're definitely here," I whispered, peering up at a gauze of cobweb in the closest of the bay windows.

I decided to park on the right side, as far away from the front of the house as I could get, and backed it up until the rear bumper poked in among the trees. If things went *really* wrong in there, I didn't want the house collapsing on top of my Ford.

Crystal got out of the truck first—and promptly shimmied out of her skirt.

Whoa. Okay, that I was *not* expecting. I blinked in astonishment at her red lace panties. She didn't seem to care one way or the other if I stared, and calmly pulled off her boots before rummaging around in her purse. As if the sight of her perfect, albeit pale legs hadn't stalled every thought in my head already, watching her pull a pair of jeans—and sneakers—from a purse too small to hold them pretty much caused a complete mental shutdown.

She hurried into them, moving like a VHS tape playing on fast forward. Before I could pick my jaw up from my lap, she had her sneakers on and appeared ready to go inside.

"What…" I gestured at her, unable to make the words work or move from the driver's seat.

Crystal stuffed her fancy boots into the purse before tossing it on the passenger seat, chucked her abandoned skirt on top of it, then shut the door. "One thing I've learned is to *always* carry a change of clothing."

"Um. Expecting you'll need to dress practical at a moment's notice?" I raised an eyebrow.

"No. I hate being stranded in the nude. Not that I'm embarrassed, but it tends to attract unwanted attention."

"Didn't think nudity bothered you."

She smiled. "It doesn't. However, when I'm trying to sneak around all inconspicuous like, it has the exact opposite effect of being unnoticed."

"How often has that happened to you?" I finally hopped out, pushed my door shut, and walked around in front of the truck.

She fell in step at my side on the way to the front porch. "Are you asking about intentional episodes, accidents, or emergencies?"

"Do I even want to know?"

Crystal grinned with a bit of shrug, like she wanted to bust out laughing—but also tried to stay quiet. "I have a few special… talents that clothes get in the way of."

"I'll bet," I muttered past a smile.

"Now whose mind is in the gutter?"

"I'm a man. My mind spends half its day there." I winked and grasped the knob.

She vanished—except for her clothes.

"Holy shit!" I hissed as quietly as possible.

She returned a few seconds later. "A perk from the fey side of the family. My great aunt's a wood nymph."

"Incredible."

"Not quite... vampires can still see me when I turn invisible. Luckily, they can't teleport."

I turned the knob and eased the door open inward. "You can teleport? Are you serious?"

"Quite. Only, it's fairly useless for anything except escaping bad situations. Only my body teleports... nothing I'm wearing or carrying goes with me. But I found a way around it, sort of. My purse isn't exactly normal."

"I kinda got that feeling already. You ready?" I asked.

"More than ready. They killed my sister."

I nodded. The problem was... I wasn't ready.

No, not at all.

Chapter Nineteen
Whacking the Nest

The door let us into a short foyer with a coat closet on both sides. Beyond it lay a large chamber with dusty-as-hell burgundy walls, sofas, and chairs. It resembled a cross between the living room of an enormous house and the common area of a hotel. The air hung thick with the smell of wet fabric and age, along with a nearly eye-watering stench of rotting corpse.

I covered my mouth and nose, stifling a cough. "Gah... do you smell that?"

"Mold?"

"No, death."

She shook her head. "No. It just smells like an abandoned building."

Whoever used to run this place as a boarding house hadn't been big on making it homey. The place had a certain sense of austerity to it, decorated in a style reminiscent of the early cheapskate period. Even before the place suffered abandonment, all the furnishings in sight looked utilitarian with little in the way of decoration. A small, round table stood between a pair of padded chairs in the corner by the hallway entrance. It held a rotary phone that probably hadn't worked—or been touched—since 1962. It honestly surprised me to see electric bulbs on the wall sconces.

Despite my newfound abilities, I still felt like a dumb rube who got drunk and tricked into whacking a hornet nest with a stick while his somewhat-less-drunk friends laughed at him. Hopefully, I won't end up screaming and running in circles.

Unfortunately, the only light source we had to work with came from the open doorway behind us. The hallway past the phone table looked exactly like the sort of pitch-black deathtrap that characters in horror movies—or any resident of Shadow Pines—should never walk down. If I had a flashlight on me, I had the distinct feeling the batteries would have died after three steps.

"You were right about it being dark," I whispered. "Guess it doesn't much matter what time we came here."

Crystal reached out her hand as if to allow a fairy to land on it; instead, a tennis-ball sized orb of yellow-green light appeared over her palm. It floated up and drifted lazily about at random, but never glided more than a few feet away from her.

Three more light spheres appeared one after the next, all dancing around in meandering paths like moths.

"Okay... guess you save a bunch of money on batteries."

She smiled. "Will-o-wisps."

"Aren't they supposed to be dark spirits that lure the unwary to drown in swamps or something?"

"That's the actual living ones. This is pure magic. And, yes, wisps can be dangerous to humans, but they're friends of the fey."

"You would never lure someone off alone into the woods, would you?"

She overacted innocence. "Never."

"But isn't that what succubi do?"

"Perhaps the full-blood versions. I'm just a harmless variant."

"How harmless?"

She winked. "Okay, maybe not that harmless."

Since I could see, I advanced into the hall, hands poised like an Old West gunslinger. Only, instead of a Colt .45—or even the Ruger .44 under my arm—I planned on reaching for something a little hotter. "Well, I hope you don't go around killing the horny bastards."

Crystal's sigh floated over my shoulder. "No. My feeding from a human only makes them a little tired. Okay, a lot tired. But trust me, they receive as much pleasure as I do. I don't know where that bit about devouring souls came from."

So much for my first impression. Guess she

isn't the type of girl who waits for marriage.

Strips of peeling wallpaper rustled in the air behind us as we went by. The dust made it hard to tell for sure, but I think the walls had once been blue with patterns in darker blue. Here and there, scraps of wooden molding lay loose along the corridor. We passed a huge dining room as well as a hall with four bathrooms. Guess when this place operated forty years ago, the boarders had to come downstairs for a shower. Everywhere I looked, things appeared to be falling apart. More interesting, nothing seemed to have been repaired, like ever. The front room had been the closest to clean, suggesting the two fiends might actually use it, but it didn't seem like they set foot anywhere else downstairs.

Not like vampires had any need of kitchens or dining rooms.

A door in the kitchen revealed steps down to a basement, heavy with the smell of mildew. Of course, I figured the vampires would be down there, but the stink of death didn't hit me as bad here. It had weakened the deeper into the house I went, so I turned around and headed back down the hall to the front room. A wide archway on my right led from there to a trash-strewn room with more sofas, tables, and bookshelves. Stairs at the back led to the second floor, and another, narrower hallway past the stairs contained closets of ancient cleaning supplies and a utility sink.

"Damn. When was the last time anyone sold

Borax?"

"What's that?" asked Crystal.

"Old cleaning stuff." I shut the closet and headed for the stairs.

"Look out, Max!"

Before I could even whirl to look at her, she grabbed me by the shirt and dragged me backward. A body sailed off the stairs above me on the right and fell in a blur to the floor. He—no doubt a vampire—bounced back to his feet before I finished stumbling into Crystal. I didn't recognize the guy. Like the other two, he appeared to be somewhere in his twenties; however, he didn't do the greaser thing. This guy had a Nirvana T-shirt and jeans on.

Red glowing eyes, fangs, and a near-total lack of color in his face made it beyond obvious I locked stares with an undead. The stench of death wafting from the guy turned my stomach as much as it filled me with the irresistible urge to destroy him—much the same way the average person reacts to having a giant cockroach appear without warning in the kitchen.

And so, as reflexively as stomping said cockroach, I reacted by thrusting my right arm out and chucking a fist-sized fireball. The dude's eyes almost shot out from their sockets. He ducked, leaving my pyrotechnic instrument of doom cruising toward the extremely dry, cobweb-covered wall behind him.

Shit.

I focused too much on dampening the flame to

react in time to the guy lunging for my throat.

Fortunately, Crystal swooped in front of me and hammered him in the jaw with her fist. My fireball hit the distant wall and whuffed out, thanks to my focused intention; still, a few scraps of flame rushed along cobwebs despite the old paper not igniting. Since I could *feel* wherever it burned, I had a fairly easy time of putting it out before disaster happened.

A rapid slapping noise came from Crystal and the vampire, like someone stuck a sirloin steak into a fan. Their arms blurred from the speed at which they traded punches and blocks... and I think the vampire had pulled a knife. Another set of footsteps came down the stairs at a run. I spun to the right, thrusting both hands out and covering the steps with a thin layer of ice.

An extremely surprised vampire woman flew ass-first down the stairway in a flailing mess of yoga pants, blue hair, and bright red claws. She slid into the room, bowling over a round wooden table between two wingback chairs, knocking it to pieces. Initially, I couldn't bring myself to attack a woman —at least until she sprang upright and pulled a gun on me.

She would've shot me right in the face, too—if Crystal hadn't thrown the other vampire into her. The bullet went past me into the wall. Time to get my head in the game. I flung my arm up and hurled a fireball at the pair. The male vampire blurred into a streak at Crystal, cornering her on the left side of the room.

The woman tried to dive out of the way, but the flames caught her arm. Like a gasoline-soaked rag, she bloomed into a standing conflagration. Her screams tore at my heart for only a moment before her voice pitch-shifted into a deep, demonic range that didn't stir any feelings of guilt.

Crystal let off a yelp of surprise and vanished straight out of her clothes, which fell to the floor as the vampire stabbed his huge knife into thin air and stumbled past where she'd been standing. Unable to stop his superhumanly fast sprint on the hardwood floor, he crashed into a bookshelf, embedding himself several inches deep in the wood with a sickening *crunch*. The poor bastard just hung there, either unconscious or in too much pain to move.

Or maybe he had some sharp bits of wood stuck into places vampires didn't much like.

I gathered some fire from the rapidly-decomposing female vampire and tossed it on the male vampire. He, too, immolated in seconds.

Crystal, naked as a forest nymph, stood beside me with her hands on her hips, shaking her head. "Sometimes, I forget how damn fast they are."

I couldn't help but stare. Her body looked far too good to be true. Perfect chest, perfect hourglass waist, perfect hips, perfect skin. "My dear, you are going to get me killed."

"You don't *have* to stare at me."

"That's like saying fire doesn't *have* to consume oxygen."

She flashed a coy smile while padding over to

her clothes, and motioned to what was left of the burning vamps. "Speaking of fire. Please don't let the house catch. We might need to go through this place with a fine toothed comb. Lots and lots of missing people's remains might be here. Plus, overgrown as it is… it would surely set off a big forest fire."

While she dressed, I concentrated on containing the flames, enough to burn the vampires without letting any of the dried-out wood ignite. Once she had her clothing back on, Crystal swiped the vampire's large hunting knife off the floor and examined it with a mild frown of disapproval.

"Something wrong?"

She tossed it and caught it by the handle. "It's a cheap knife with no balance. I prefer throwing knives as they let me keep some distance. Now that I think about it, I should really pick archery back up. Assuming I could find wooden arrows some-where."

"Pick it *back* up?"

"College sports."

"Oh. Thought it might've been a fey thing."

She smiled. "No, the fey thing is the attraction to knives over guns."

The flames engulfing both vampires died down, leaving black ash piles. Even their bones had disint-egrated to powder. Only fragments of their shoes remained. When I no longer sensed any active combustion, I turned my attention to the stairs.

"How many do you think there are?"

She cocked her head, one ear toward the stairs in silence for a few seconds. "Three or four more... plus some humans."

"You can tell that by listening? Humans I mean?"

"Vampires wouldn't be begging someone to let them go and not kill them."

"Dammit. Let's go!"

Chapter Twenty
Reinforcements... Almost

I ran up the stairs, both forgetting entirely about the ice I'd covered them with and also not affected by it. Interesting... I'm walking on ice and not sliding because I don't want to. Crystal enjoyed no such relationship with slipperiness. She does, however, evidently have claws—which she used to hold on to the wall and banister.

And yeah, something was definitely switched in me. This girl's fingernails have become four-inch daggers and seeing it didn't freak me out at all. She still looked like an angel who'd gotten into a deadly situation way over her head, only the nervous fear I saw in her wide eyes wasn't actual fear. It came purely from me interpreting her normal appearance that way. Nothing about her body language said she had the least bit of fear. If anything, it said she's pissed at me for leaving the ice on the stairs.

She did have a point there. If we needed to make a quick exit, going face-first down the stairs would be inconvenient.

I dispelled the inch-thick layer into fog. She emitted a nearly inaudible sigh of thanks. When I reached the top, the glow from her will-o-wisp lights let me see a fair distance into the corridor. Predictably for a boarding house, it had a ton of doors. The second and third floor are likely all bedrooms. Though, a portion of the third floor could be a full apartment for the owner. This place ceased operating as a boarding house before I was born.

Soft thumping came from the ceiling along with murmuring voices too faint to make out words. Sounded like people on the third floor. An eerie mist hovered above the dark blue carpet leading down the second floor hall, the smell of rotting meat so strong I could scarcely take a breath without gagging. Following the sound, I continued up to the third floor.

When I'd reached about three-quarters of the way to the top, Crystal appeared out of thin air on the stairs in front of me, once again in her birthday suit. A loud *click* of teeth came from behind me. I whirled around and jumped at the sight of a vampire hugging her empty shirt, having chomped down on nothing.

Before I could even think 'burn it,' Crystal tore a four-foot-long piece of banister off and threw it over my shoulder like a spear, piercing the vampire's chest and pinning him to the wall at the bottom of the stairs.

"Ooh!" She fumed and stomped—putting her foot *through* the old step. She had the grace and reflexes to not fall over, or even stumble, or even look like she hadn't expected it to break out from under her. "That is *so* rude. Grabbing a lady from behind like that."

The vampire hung from the banister pinning him to the wall, gripping it in both hands and struggling to pull it loose. Her shot had dipped too low to hit him in the heart, but it didn't seem like he'd be going anywhere soon. Not bothering to wait and see if he could free himself, I did the only reasonable thing a guy could do in this situation.

I lit him on fire.

Crystal scooted past me to retrieve her clothes, which lay draped on the stairs. "He came out of nowhere and grabbed me from behind."

"The mist on the second floor," I muttered. "He'd been waiting to ambush us."

"Oh, dammit. I don't even know why I'm bothering to get dressed again."

"Because people don't walk around in their birthday suits."

"I should just move to Wales and prance around the forests. My ancestors had the right idea."

"So stay naked. You won't hear me complaining."

She smirked. "I can't. You'll die, right?"

"Is that what they mean by 'drop dead gorgeous'?"

That got a laugh out of her. "Close, you silly goose. You'll be staring at me and a vampire will rip your head off."

"You know, that whole 'so scared she jumped out of her clothes' thing is supposed to be a joke."

"For your information..." She pointed at me, bra hanging from her hand. "I was not scared. Jumping up the stairs was the best way for me to get out of being grabbed."

"Didn't you say something about your blood being poisonous to them? Why not let him bite you and learn the error of his ways the hard way?"

She slipped into her bra and shirt blurrily fast. "Because, then I'd have a bite wound. Unlike vampires, *I* don't magically heal in ten seconds."

"Oh."

Crystal swiped her jeans off the floor and put them on. "Takes me more like an hour."

"Oh, is that all." There might have been sarcasm in my voice.

"And being bitten still hurts, smarty pants. A lot." She sat to put her sneakers on.

As soon as she jumped to her feet, I continued into the hallway upstairs. Out of habit, I drew my . 44. It wouldn't kill a vampire, but it should at least have enough punch to stagger one for a few seconds. Enough to buy me time to start a fire. Crystal grabbed another two pieces of banister, each about a foot long, and used her claws to sharpen them into points, flicking wood shavings off the tips like she peeled carrots... with her finger.

Wow, sexy and badass.

Grunting came from the third door on the left. I stepped up to it, steeled myself, and burst in all cop-style, giant revolver raised in both hands.

The room contained two twin beds, one against the wall on either side, both with people in shredded college sweatshirts and jeans tied down by thin chain and padlocks around each wrist and ankle. The girl on the left lifted her head off the pillow to stare at me with faintly glowing eyes. Barely twenty if even that, she looked like death warmed over. The boy on the other bed, around the same age, had a football player's jersey on and didn't appear fully conscious. He, too, had pronounced grey in his skin, though his eyes didn't light up—they didn't even focus. Straight in front of me, a skinny blonde cheerleader type in a peach shift dress, barefoot, sat chained by the neck to an ancient freestanding radiator. She still had the color of a living person to her, though quite a bit of blood had soaked into the shoulders of her dress.

"Help!" shouted the blonde. "Please let me out of here."

I eyed the two on the beds… and started raising my hands, fireballs already forming.

"Wait." Crystal grasped my arm. "They're not fully gone yet."

"Huh?"

"They're still tied down. That means they haven't turned completely. It's not permanent until they've fed for the first time. If we destroy the vampire who gave them the three bites before they drink, they should recover."

"Should. What if they don't?"

"Then we'll... figure something out. Not all vampires are like Derek and Piper, ya know."

"Could have fooled me."

Right on cue, another vampire emerged from a doorway about thirty feet farther down the hall—and pointed an AR-15 at us. I summoned a thick slab of stone in front of me as a shield and tossed a fireball around it. Crystal whirled around and threw one of her stakes. The vamp with the rifle fired, the report deafening in the closed confines of the hallway. My stone barrier withstood the bullets, even if the floor under it emitted scary cracking noises at the weight. My first fireball missed, but made him flinch enough that I had time to concentrate on igniting the air around him.

A squishy *thump* came from behind me at the same moment the AR-15 vampire burst into flames. I peered back past Crystal at a female vampire a bit older looking than the others I'd seen so far, laying inert on the floor about twelve feet away with a stake embedded in her chest, twitching like a fish out of water. She went still after a few seconds and dried out into a pile of clothing and grey powder.

"You gotta get us out of here," said the girl chained to the bed. "They're gonna kill us."

I swiveled to face her, but before I could think of what to do, another woman screamed in terror from down the hall. "Hold that thought." I pointed at her. "Be back in a moment."

"No! Don't leave us here!" shouted the girl while struggling.

"Hey!" yelled Radiator Girl, running to the end of her leash. "Don't go!"

Yeah, walking away from three kidnap victims might've been a dick move. Ask Justine. I'm good at pulling dick moves. Though, she tended to call me an asshole more than a dick. Anyway, I didn't quite trust that those three were as harmless as they claimed. At least not yet. I suspected it would've been more of a dick move to get close enough for them to kill me, thus condemning them to undeath.

In the hallway, I stopped a few steps from the door the scream came from and hurled a conjured rock at it. Not too big a rock, only the size of a watermelon. Plenty big enough to take the door out. The instant it smashed its way into the room, a flurry of gunfire erupted from within.

"Shit!" shouted Piper.

Since I'm sure they could hear me even if I whispered, I glanced at Crystal with a look I hoped she read as 'if we step into that doorway, we're going to be riddled with bullets.'

She turned invisible for a second, then reappeared, pointing at her eyes, then at the wall. Oh, damn. That's right. She said the vampires could still see her. Hmm. This blew.

I blinked.

Blew...

Idea!

Chapter Twenty-One
Wind and Fury

Crystal reacted to the shift in my expression from confused to devilish grin by dropping into a stance. She looked ready to charge in the door as soon as I did something.

And do something I did.

I raised my arms, palms up, and called the wind, pushing it into the room. Streamers of rotting wallpaper peeled off the walls and went flying. Paintings sailed, small tables collapsed, little vases smashed.

"What the fuck is this?" yelled Derek over the gale.

A woman screamed again.

I lifted my hands higher, increasing the force of the blast. More paper, and some plaster bits, ripped off the walls on either side of me. A sconce or three went flying as well, lightbulbs shattering. Crystal might have amazing reflexes, but she didn't weigh that much. She flew into me from behind and wrapped her arms around me, sheltering inside the small area of calm at the eye of the storm I'd made.

Bangs and crashes came from the room along with the tinkle of smashing glass. Daylight burst into the corridor, no doubt from the hurricane tearing the boards off the windows. Hundred-mile-per-hour winds weren't meant to exist inside a house. The same woman emitted a yowl of pain. At the *thud* of a body hitting the floor, I decided to roll the dice and charged through the door.

The large bedroom looked like… well, it looked like a tornado tore it apart. Both windows were little more than rectangular openings in the wall, now with no glass or curtains. Two bright beams of sunlight slanted into the room. Papers and trash still fluttered in the air over a single queen-sized bed, along with glittering dust motes. Piper's legs stuck up from a pile of smashed furniture at the far left corner. I figured he took a marble-topped table straight to the face. Closer on the right, Derek stood beside another college-age woman with red hair. Her little green dress, runny makeup, and earrings told me she'd went out for a fun night and found the exact opposite. Fortunately, I didn't see any blood on or near her neck, but they'd cuffed her hands behind her back, tethering her by a six-foot chain to another radiator.

These two seriously got on my nerves.

A handgun sat on the rug within lunging reach of Derek. The instant his squinting gaze shifted from me to the gun, I covered it in ice, freezing it in place on the floor. He zipped behind the redhead and stared at me intently. Dark crimson light glowed from deep within his eyes in time with a sudden upwelling of the strong urge to destroy him. His cocky grin faltered to worry. As if by magic, a hunting knife appeared in his hand, held to her throat.

"What the hell is going on?" shouted Derek.

The young woman squirmed, equal parts furious and terrified. "You kidnapped me, you asshole! That's what's going on. Get off me!"

"Game over, man." I said, raising my hands.

"You... you just stand right there and let Piper end your ass, or I'm gonna kill this bitch." Again Derek's eyes glowed, and my anger grew. A small tug at my temples told me he'd been trying to pry his way into my thoughts. This was his attempt to control me, but it didn't work. And thank God it didn't.

Piper groaned and pulled himself out of the pile of furniture pieces. Crystal slipped in behind me, still holding the stake she made from the railing.

I waved my hand, and the gentle nudging at my temples disappeared. "That's not much incentive for me. Didn't Justine tell you? I'm an asshole... among other things." I wagged my eyebrows. "Besides, you were going to kill that young woman anyway. You're really bad at negotiation."

The redhead pushed herself up on tiptoe, trying to move her throat away from the blade. Derek's eyes glowed, and my anger grew. I literally saw myself smashing his face in with something... fist, rock, block of ice, whatever.

"Get on the floor," snarled Piper while staring at me, along with a flash of glow in his eyes. I felt another nudge at my temples. Yeah, I was supposed to get on the floor, per his telepathic command. Except, of course, his mind tricks didn't work on me.

And now I wanted to smash his face in, too.

"It don't work on him," rasped Derek. He shifted his stare to Crystal and his eyes pulsed with the crimson light of his mental powers. "Kill that asshole. And when you're done, kill yourself, too."

"I don't feel like it." She shook her head. "I kinda like the guy. And I kinda like me, too, for that matter."

Piper rubbed his forehead. "You idiot. Why are you even trying that on her? You know what she is."

"What the hell is going on?" whispered the redhead.

Both vampires shouted, "Shut up!" at the same time, though Derek added 'bitch.'

"Hey, don't be mean to her." Crystal wagged the stake at him.

"I think they're well past the point of mean... unless she's into being handcuffed and chained to a radiator, which I doubt."

Derek glanced to his right at Piper with an 'is

this guy for real?' expression.

The instant he looked away from me, I conjured as much water as I could, lifting a standing wall of it about seven feet high before projecting it forward at Derek and the college girl. They both went over backward from the force of the impact. Piper leapt into a sprint at me, but Crystal chucked the stake at him. A split second before it perforated his heart, he blocked, winding up with a stake impaling his left forearm.

I tossed a fireball on Derek, but his soaked clothes prevented him from igniting. The redhead threw herself away from him, rolling to the side as best she could while still chained.

Wood didn't exist in my talent set, but I could do stone. Unfortunately, being on the third floor of a house put me kinda far from the earth, which made calling stone exhausting. That bullet shield in the hallway damn near made me want to sleep. Damn. Ice time. I made grabbing motions toward the carpet, gathering some of the loose water up into a rapidly-freezing spear-shaped lance—that I rammed through Derek, pinning him to the floor.

"Nice," said Crystal.

I grunted. "Learned that from you... on the stairs."

Dark blood foamed out of the cocky bastard's mouth past his extended fangs. He emitted a roar too deep to come from anything human. Piper yanked the stake out of his arm, tossed it aside, and tried to run at me again. Crystal got in his way, and for the second time today, I witnessed a punching match that looked like a Kung Fu movie played at four times speed. Only, this time, Crystal had a clear advantage in both speed and strength due to the daylight streaming into the room. She basically beat the ever loving shit out of him, only her punches didn't appear to cause much damage.

The redhead scrambled onto her knees, then stood, running to the end of the chain like she expected she might be able to pull the radiator up from the floor. Alas, she couldn't. But with her now safely away from Derek, who remained pinned to the floor, I concentrated on throwing fire at him. That is, until he pushed himself upward… one problem with an *ice* lance: it melts and it's slippery. Okay, that's two problems.

He twisted himself to the right hard enough to snap the frozen shaft… and I decided to stop being an idiot.

I commanded all the water saturating his clothes to spray off him in an explosion of vapor.

Now dry, Derek started to scream, "No!" but it melted into a demonic howl of agony as I covered him with flames.

Piper abruptly sped himself up, catching Crystal with a right hook to the jaw that she couldn't get away from. The hit didn't bother her *too* much, though it did make her stagger backward a few steps and growl. While Derek thrashed and burned on the floor, Piper sprinted into a smear of T-shirt and jeans. He plowed into Crystal, body-blocking her so hard she flew off her feet and smacked into the wall. The bastard didn't bother slowing down or looking back, running out into the hall.

"Shit!" gasped Crystal as she fell and bounced off a dresser to the floor.

The redhead finally noticed Derek burning down into a molten clump of black goop. Much to my surprise, she didn't scream, merely stared. "Umm. What the hell am I looking at?"

Ignoring her, Crystal snarled and dashed out the door, chasing Piper.

"That's a dead vampire," I answered.

"I figured as much. So, what does that make you?"

I grinned. "Someone who's not a fan of vampires. Wait here."

She rattled her chains. "Do I have a choice?"

I winked. "Be back in a sec. One of them is getting away."

"Hey, that was a rhetorical question!" she yelled after me. "You can't leave me here, you asshole! And where did all that wind come from?"

Except, of course, I had already sprinted out the door after Crystal.

Following the tromping of footsteps, I raced down the stairs to the ground floor. Crystal wasn't quite as fast on her feet as the vampires, but damn, the girl could move way faster than I had any hope of going. She'd gotten out of sight by the time I made it to the main hallway, though my gut told me they'd gone down the basement steps.

Hmm. Why the hell would Piper go to the basement? Oh... maybe so I can't knock out another window board and weaken him. I scrambled after them as fast as I could down the rickety wooden stairs. One good thing about that vampire being tall, he ate all the cobwebs.

A loud *thud* with a strange energetic buzzing twang echoed up from below.

Crystal grunted like she'd flown into another wall.

I rushed to the bottom of the stairs and skidded to a stop at the sight of a wide column of green light a short distance in front of me, surrounding Crystal. Wisps moved within the energy, like smoke passing through a laser. She pounded at the other side, evidently trapped inside a force field about eight feet across. Paint on the floor outlined the area of the circle along with various indecipherable squiggles and writings I couldn't even identify the language of, much less read.

No sign of Piper, who must've kept going deeper into the basement. Crystal's will-o-wisp still hovered close to her, also trapped inside the... whatever. Walking into a pitch black basement to hunt a vampire without any light source sounded like an exceedingly stupid idea.

Even for me.

"Damn." Crystal kicked at the barrier. "Wasn't expecting anything like this."

"Crimony biscuits," I muttered.

"Shit." Crystal bonked her head against the

force field.

"Sorry... didn't mean to make you think of her."

Crystal whirled to face me. "No, it's not that. Dana must've found out about someone in the family turning against me, but they killed her before she could warn me."

"You're saying this whole thing was a trap for *you*?"

She squatted, examining the floor. "Doubtful. This is too hastily made. I'm sure they only meant to kill her to keep her quiet, but when I hired you..."

"Those two nitwits led us right here... and into a trap."

"Or at least set this up on the off chance I came with you."

I pressed a hand against the energy wall, smooth as glass, neither warm nor cold.

Crystal abruptly grabbed her chest and collapsed to one knee, grimacing in pain.

"Shit. What happened?"

She took a few rapid, shallow breaths. "Can't teleport out."

Piper's haughty laughter drifted out of the shadows.

I let my arm drop and walked around the column. "Be right back."

"Wait... it's dark. He'll be all over you if you can't see him."

Arms raised to either side, I surrounded myself in swirling tendrils of fire that swam around and around me like flying serpents. "I can do light, too."

She pressed herself against the barrier, staring at me like a young wife watching her new husband sail off to World War II, knowing she'd never see him again.

Or maybe she just had that kinda face.

"Be right back."

"Careful!" whispered Crystal.

Hands clenched into fists, I stalked into the darkness.

Chapter Twenty-Two
Pay the Piper

The beeping of cell phone buttons came from a narrow stone archway up ahead.

Flickering orange light from my dancing flame serpents reflected from pale brick walls covered in dusty cobwebs. I walked toward the noise in the slow, deliberate gait of a horror-movie killer. I wasn't trying to be ominous, merely careful. Though, as angry as I'd become, maybe I threw off some intense vibes. The archway led to a room lined with empty wine racks—and one agitated greaser vampire.

To be extra sure he didn't get away, I summoned a stone slab to grow up from the floor, blocking the arch behind me, and thickened it to about eight inches. He's not getting past me... and if I die, he'll be stuck in here for a long damn time.

"You guys should lay off the hair products. No wonder you turn into fireballs so fast."

Piper nearly dropped his phone, stared at me for an instant, then dashed off deeper into the basement. I moved up to a jog, following him into the next room, which held an old rust bomb of a furnace. The place still had a coal chute at the far end. He hadn't quite made it halfway to it before I covered the chute with another sudden conjuration of stone.

He skidded to a stop, gawking at the liquefied rock solidifying before him. "Blast… where the hell are they?"

"Not sure who *they* are, but I can tell you that they're not going to show up fast enough to make a difference for you."

"Wait." He faced me, backing up. "This isn't what we agreed on. They were supposed to be here, not leave me to die." He seemed to be talking himself.

"You're already dead."

He blinked, looked at me. "Now is really not the time for semantics."

I stepped closer, petting the orbiting fire serpents like actual living creatures. Yeah, maybe I hammed it up a bit, but I didn't think many people could scare vampires the way they so often terrified humans. Speaking of terrified humans, I'd left four of them upstairs. Probably shouldn't dawdle. I thrust my arm out and one of the fire serpents took off like a spear at Piper.

He blurred to the side, dodging the relatively

slow projectile with ease. "Wait. Hear me out. We don't need to be enemies, Max. I'm not even all that upset you destroyed Derek. He was too reckless, too violent. One of this town's founding families is trying to capture that... creature who hired you."

"We figured that out already. And it's a bit hypocritical of you to call anyone else a creature." I sent another fire serpent at him, trying to will it to fly faster. It rocketed forward at about the same speed as a baseball pitch.

Piper still glided out of the way like he didn't even have to work at it. "Yes, but do you know which family it is?"

"Her own, of course. Or at least the mortal half."

"Not quite." Piper held up a finger. "It's the Farringtons. I don't know exactly what they want her for, but I don't imagine it will end well for her. I'd be quite happy to offer you whatever assistance I'm capable of in exchange for not killing me."

I narrowed my eyes, contemplating the odds of this not being a lie. He had been the more pleasant of the two, but that didn't say much. He didn't have any problem with Dana's murder, killing me, or doing... whatever they did to those people upstairs. Still, having him on our side might be an advantage too good to throw away. Question was, could I trust him?

His gradually sneaking a hand behind his back answered much sooner than I expected with a resounding 'no.'

I lifted my arm as if to rub my chin in thought, but thrust it forward with the desire to call lightning. A blindingly bright shaft of white energy connected my outstretched fingers to his chest in an instant, along with a painfully loud *kaboom*. A knife went flying off to the side, thrown by an involuntary convulsion from the electrical charge coursing through him. Momentary paralysis bought me the two seconds it took for all four of my fire serpents to engulf him. He collapsed, shrieking in agony. The skin of his face split open, revealing a fanged skull that charred to black in mere seconds. A bony arm reached out of the blaze toward me.

Sudden apprehension made me back up several steps.

Piper exploded in a shower of flaming globules of bloody slime, littering the area around him with dozens of individual fires. Only the ceiling consisted of wood, everything else either stone or concrete... so I didn't need to force any flames out. I stood there watching him burn until the room returned to complete darkness.

"I've contemplated your offer, and, I'm sorry to say, I don't think there's any real possibility for trust between us."

To no great surprise, Piper didn't say anything. Just sat there looking, well... ashen.

The stink of death left the air. Only the smell of overcooked steak hung in the basement. That and a moldy wet dirt odor. Hmph. When I conjured a handful of fire to see, a glint caught my eye. Turned out to be a set of keys with a BMW symbol on the fob sticking out of the dust Piper had left behind. That might come in handy. I pocketed the key and made my way back to the larger room where Crystal paced around inside the magical prison like a fairy in a bottle. Heh. She technically *was* a fey in a bottle. Just not a tiny one. She brightened at the sight of me, but her smile didn't last long. She punched the energy wall, which created an odd buzzing noise from the transparent field.

"Did you find him?"

I nodded. "Ashes."

"Good."

"Now what?" I asked.

"Still trying to come up with something." She scowled at the painted markings.

"Better do it quick," I said. "I think we're going to have company soon."

Chapter Twenty-Three
Reprieve

"The *Farringtons?*" she screamed, once I finished explaining what Piper said. "Are you serious?"

"Yeah. At least, that's what he said. Could've been lying... though I didn't really get that feeling from him. That, and he went for a knife. No sense lying to a guy you're intending to kill."

"Great." She looked around at her glowing enclosure. "I ran into this thing like a complete idiot. Now what? I guess I just sit here until the Farringtons come to collect me? Ugh."

"Don't you know the rules?" I smirked. "The dame who gets involved with a private eye is almost always kidnapped."

Crystal frowned. "Real life isn't a cliché... and why did you call me a 'dame?'"

I shrugged. "Going with the shtick."

She resumed pacing.

"However... I'm going to try and change the script," I said. "I don't really want you to be kidnapped. Or killed, since this is real life and all."

"Great. I don't like either one of those options, either. So, umm, what are you planning to do, Mr. Detective? Stick around and shoot icicles at anyone who tries to kidnap me?"

I studied the floor, eyeballing the stone under me. After some quick visualization, I widened my stance and projected my willpower into the earth, pushing rock and soil aside. A bowl formed between my feet, deepening in response to my desires. It grew to a pit as wide as a phone booth, then burrowed downward. I opened a passage like a giant U-bend from a sink drain, bringing the other end up into the area walled off by magic.

Directly under Crystal.

Oops.

She fell, but caught herself on the edge, armpit deep in the floor. As soon as she realized what I'd done, she let go. As if afraid the tunnel would close at any second, she scrambled up out the other end as I stepped aside, covered in dirt, but overjoyed. She even hugged me.

"Now for the hard part," I muttered.

"Dealing with the Farringtons?"

"No. I'm hoping we can get out of here before they show up. I meant those people upstairs. If destroying Piper and Derek—and the other vampires in this place—didn't break the curse on them, we're going to have to put them down, too."

"Oh. Yeah." She sighed. "That sucks. But we won't necessarily have to destroy them. While I admit it's the most likely outcome, there's no *guarantee* they'll be evil. We should hurry, I can hear that one girl screaming her head off."

"Which one?"

"I think it's the redhead. She sounds angry. Her father must be in the Navy."

"How can you tell?" I asked.

"Just making a sailor joke. She's swearing up a storm." Crystal hurried to the stairs. "Can't say I blame her. I'd be pissed off if someone chained me to a radiator, too... not that they could."

"Oh? Okay, I have to ask..." I jogged up behind her.

"I have a way with locks."

"You're just full of surprises."

She laughed. "You have no idea."

"What else can you do?"

Crystal dashed across the house to the stairs in the front room. "Wings."

"Okay, I know that one."

"But you haven't seen them."

"I can't say I have."

"Then be prepared to be surprised... someday."

"I'll be as prepared as possible. Do you have a tail, too?"

"Nope."

The redhead's continuous screamed curses—mostly calling me an asshole among other things—

reached my ears when I'd made it halfway to the second floor. When we reached the third, I shouted, "Hang on! Be right there."

She stopped yelling, but did fire off a, "Hurry the hell up, dickwad!"

We stopped at the first room with the three prisoners in it. I nearly fell over in relief at seeing them back to normal, no longer halfway to undead. The effect of the change also knocked all three of them out cold. I did a quick pulse check, confirming that they all remained alive. None of them gave off a deathly smell, either.

"They're good," I reported.

"You're sure?" asked Crystal, a note of suspicion in her eyes.

"Yeah. No stink like death and… look at them. They have their color back. Don't suppose you have any idea how long they'll stay unconscious?"

"Nope."

She grasped one of the padlocks securing the woman's wrist, and pulled it open like it hadn't even been locked. A tiny spritz of what I could only call 'fairy dust' shot out of the keyhole. Wow, no wonder this girl is doing okay for herself. Her kind would make amazing thieves. Can turn invisible, open any lock they want… granted, she'd have to break into a place bare-assed and anything she carried out would still show up on camera, but… no one would be able to tell *who* broke in.

Hmm. I wonder if succubi leave fingerprints?

One by one, she opened all nine padlocks, four

each for the guy and girl on the bed, one on the woman tethered to the radiator. We jogged down the hall to the other bedroom. The redhead contin-ued trying to either snap the chain or tear the radiator off its bolts.

"Hey, calm down. You're going to hurt your-self," I said.

She shot me a look that could've scorched the paint off a battleship. Maybe I shouldn't have told her to calm down. "You left me here!"

"Had a vampire to destroy. If he got away, he would've done this to someone else."

The woman huffed. "Did you at least get him?"

"Yep."

Crystal breezed in and walked around behind her. "Found the key in the other ash pile. What's your name?"

"Shiloh Morgan. Did someone send you to find me?"

"Not specifically," I said. "Came here looking for vampires. How long have you been missing for?"

A magical spark flew off the handcuffs and they popped open.

"Only a few days." Shiloh pulled her arms around in front and rubbed her chafed wrists. "They left me in here like this the whole time. I think they were biting the others. Or drinking, or whatever the hell it is that vampires do."

"I can confirm that... but they're okay now." I fished out the BMW key and tossed it to her. "Here.

He won't be needing it anymore. Cops probably won't let you keep it, but it'll get you back home."

She nodded. "What about the others?"

"Might take your friends a bit to wake up."

She glanced down at the key in her hand, then back to me. "Wait. Why?"

"A little while ago when I said they were going to kill you anyway, I think I might have unintentionally lied. I don't think *they* were going to kill you. They'd been keeping you here to give to your friends as their first meal. All three of them were most of the way to becoming vampires. Guess someone wanted reinforcements."

Shiloh gasped. "No... they're dead?"

"Nah." Crystal patted her on the shoulder. "Pretty damn close, but we killed the one who'd bitten them... and since your friends hadn't yet fed, the curse didn't set in. Not sure how long they'll be out of it, but they're probably going to need a trip to the hospital. All of them are low on blood."

"Might as well carry them outside," I said with a shrug.

Crystal lifted her head as if listening to something. "We should get out of here right now. Shiloh, find somewhere to hide until it's clear."

"What?" I asked.

"At least two vehicles are coming." Crystal dashed for the bedroom door. "Come on."

Shiloh ran after us down the hallway, but ducked into the room with her friends instead of following us down the stairs. As soon as the door shut, Crystal returned and did something with the lock.

She grinned. "My magic works both ways. Not only will this door not open until I return, the bad guys won't see the door."

"Red won't like it."

"Nope, but she will be alive when we return for her." And with that, my new and very beautiful friend raced off again.

I hauled ass, trying my best to keep up with Crystal as she ran down two flights of stairs, across the ground floor, and out the front door. A black Cadillac sedan with a red pickup truck following it crept up the dirt road and they both had trouble written all over them. They'd written it in all capitals on the truck, as it carried six or seven guys in the bed with rifles.

"Hang on." I stopped on the porch. "They're gonna pick us off if we run for my truck. I'll give us some cover."

Since I had no idea who might be in that car or what the Farringtons may or may not be involved with, tipping my proverbial hand as anything more than an ordinary private investigator was unwise. I closed my eyes, trying to infuse the air with water vapor without using flashy hand motions. In my mind's eye, I pictured the lot in front of the boarding house, all the trees, the weeds, and everything vanishing behind a thick layer of white fog.

"Wow. That's so creepy. You did it. Come on."

Crystal pulled at my arm.

I opened my eyes to a fog so thick I couldn't see six feet away. It's possible they didn't notice us on the covered porch, but they definitely would've seen us running across the lot. Now, we ran blind into the mist, in as best a guess as I could remember to where I parked. Crystal held my hand, for once following me. Whether my senses detected the weight of the truck upon the earth or the large collection of metal in front of me pulled me toward it, I made my way to my Ford with relative accuracy—and only stumbled on weeds three times.

We got in together, pulling the doors closed as quietly as possible. Crystal hunkered down, sitting on the floor while I slipped the key in the ignition. I didn't trust my memory enough to attempt driving in fog this thick, especially with two cars coming in the only road out. The shouts of men complaining about the mist passed by in front of us. Most blamed the vampires for it while one felt certain 'that some other weird shit' caused it.

Confident they no longer stood between us and the way out, I cranked the ignition, cut the wheel to the left, and accelerated while simultaneously commanding the fog in front of me to form a tunnel of clear air. It worked well enough that I managed to swerve and prevent crashing into a stray tree that had invaded the parking area.

"Hey, there they go!" shouted a guy behind us.

"Where?"

"Shoot out the tires!"

"I can't see shit."

"Uh oh," said Crystal.

"Yeah… 'uh oh' is right."

The sound of a few car door slams came from behind.

I couldn't concentrate on thickening the fog behind us while driving, so I decided to make a run for it. The far end of the mist tunnel revealed a wall of impassable trees. Out of desperation, I commanded all the fog in front of us to condense into rain, which cleared the air and let me find the road… about fifteen feet to the right of where I'd been steering. My truck handled pretty well for an old war horse, and didn't roll over on me at the hard swerve. Once on the road—or what attempted to be one—I accelerated to about forty.

Crystal popped up to peer backward. "The truck went into some trees, but the car made it to the road. He's not going too fast. We're leaving him behind."

"That thing doesn't have the shocks for a rough trail like this. Hopefully it'll buy us enough time to get out to the pavement and haul ass for town."

My new succubi friend looked over at me. "Max… don't take this into town or they'll get the police involved."

"So? Wouldn't we kinda want them involved?"

"The cops are under their control. They'll arrest us both and make up whatever story they want."

"That's a bit much. The vampires aren't control-ling *every* cop. And if they could do that, why didn't they grab you the day you confronted Justine about the shoddy investigation into Dana's death?"

"I'm quite difficult to kidnap, and they know that. At least, with anything the police have access to. They wouldn't have been able to hold me long enough for the Farringtons to pick me up."

"True. But wouldn't whoever set this up expect killing Dana would get you involved, bring you out of Ironside?"

She rolled her eyes. "That's *exactly* what they wanted. I'm sure they killed her primarily to lure me away from Ironside. They knew I'd come back here at least for her funeral. It's far more difficult for them to do anything over there. In short, they could set up a trap here."

"Any idea why they want you dead or captured?"

"No idea, other than I don't play by their rules... and I know most of their secrets."

"Your sister probably rejected their ways, too."

"Hard to say. I think she mostly went along, until..."

"Until she heard of the Farringtons' plans to execute you."

"Or imprison me, but yeah."

"Okay. Well, it's a good thing I don't have a cat."

"Say again?"

I grinned. "Don't have to worry about not feeding him if I don't make it back home tonight. To Ironside it is. But, if you want to avoid town, we'll need to take the long way around."

"Take whatever way around you want," said Crystal, eyeing the side mirror. "Just do it faster… they're gaining on us."

Sure enough, a black Cadillac Sedan and a red Dodge pickup emerged from the trees behind us, racing around a bend in the road.

"Crap. Hold on."

Chapter Twenty-Four
Obligatory

I accelerated up to sixty... not the wisest thing to do on a backwoods road riddled with holes, rocks, and curves.

Whoever drove the Cadillac handled the car pretty damn well for the terrain, managing to keep up with us. The truck lagged a little ways behind... and for the time being, the bumpiness of the road kept the guys in the open bed clinging for their lives rather than trying to get a shot at us. One or two raised their rifles, but either the trees got in the way on a bend or their truck bounced over something hard enough that they worried more about not going flying than trying to fire at us.

"They're chasing us," said Crystal, oddly calm.

"Yeah, it's in the rules. Just like the pretty girl who gets involved with a PI ends up kidnapped?

There's gotta be a car chase."

She flashed this cute smile at me that made my heart do bad things. Well, good things, but palpitations in the midst of a car chase are kinda bad.

"Wonder how much they're paying those idiots," I muttered while nearly losing control on a sliding left turn.

"They could be vampires... falling out of a truck at this speed would be more annoying than deadly." She peered out at the sky. "It'll be dark in less than an hour. This could get messy if we don't make it to Ironside."

I debated going faster, but didn't trust the truck's ability to stay on the road or avoid rolling. Doing sixty-five here already well exceeded my comfort level. "Why are you so convinced they'll leave us alone if we make it there?"

"Two reasons. First—" She yelped and grabbed the roof handles, clinging for dear life as I hurled the truck into a sliding right turn when the road decided to go all hairpin on me unexpectedly.

Branches hammered the roof and side of my truck like a Neal Peart drum solo for a few seconds before we skidded back onto the road. Both the Caddy and the Dodge chasing us decided to hit their brakes hard for the same curve. My driving like an idiot bought us about sixty yards of distance.

"First," said Crystal, giving me an intense 'you're not supposed to kill us either' stare, "The families don't have anywhere near the same amount of influence there. They haven't bothered infiltrating the police, town council, or mayor's office as deeply. Second... there's a ton of werewolves."

I damn near stomped on the brakes to take my chances with the guys behind us... but didn't. "Werewolves?"

"Don't sound so incredulous. You're fully aware that vampires exist. You have magic, and you've met me." She sprouted her horns long enough to wink at me.

If anyone had ever asked me if I'd have considered a girl with little curved ram horns adorable, I'd have laughed and probably made a joke about people doing illegal drugs. But... somehow, they worked for her. And yes, adorable.

"Great. Werewolves."

"Relax. They won't give you any problems at all. They're big on nature, too."

"Are you serious?"

"Yeah. You know, *wolves*? They're nature spirits."

"What about that full moon stuff? Murder sprees?"

She pointed at the rear window. "They're getting closer. And I dunno. I've never heard of a werewolf seriously losing their mind at a full moon. They revere the Moon as a force of nature. It's probably vampires giving them bad PR."

I couldn't help but laugh at that—but not the 'they're getting closer' part. The truck had taken the lead, better able to cope with the rough road than the Caddy. Of course, as car chases went, we basically sped along at the equivalent of a lazy Sunday drive. Sixty MPH didn't make for breakneck speeds on a freeway, but on back country lanes, I expected death to leap out at us any second.

The *crack* of a rifle startled an F-bomb out of me and made Crystal yell in surprise.

So much for slowing down. The narrow road with thick trees on both sides didn't offer me much room to evade gunfire, and constant blind curves ahead made the idea of going into the oncoming lane about as fun as a game of Russian roulette. This area didn't exactly have a lot of traffic, but it would be just my luck that the one other car on the road within fifty miles would show up as soon as I strayed out of the lane.

More gunfire went off behind us in an urgent, albeit random peppering. Nothing—as far as I could tell—hit us. I swerved randomly between lanes on a maybe quarter-mile stretch when the firing intensified. There, I picked it up to about ninety.

Crystal screamed as I slammed on the brakes ahead of a hard left turn. Something—branch or bullet I couldn't tell—clanked off the truck bed. Fading daylight made the road even more treacherous. If I hadn't spent most of my life driving around this area, I'd have been scared shitless. Though, the approaching darkness *did* make us a harder target to shoot.

Unless they were vampires...

Trees flashed by in the glare of my headlights, bullets whistled overhead, and time blurred. Some part of my brain knew it would take us about a half hour to circle Shadow Pines on the outskirts and reach the highway connecting to Ironside. I called it a highway, but around here, that only meant it had been paved and didn't have too many curves. And the half-hour estimate also included driving like a sane person.

The road ahead of us straightened out for about two miles… and the forest receded back, leaving us out in the open.

Crap. We're going to be sitting ducks. "Take the wheel."

Crystal glanced at me with an 'are you serious?' face for only a second or two before she climbed into my lap and grabbed the steering wheel. Good thing she's thin.

Distracting as that was, I managed to slide out from under her and crawl into the passenger seat, where I faced backwards. Using my newfound abilities on people bothered me, but I've never been a big fan of body piercings and I certainly didn't want one from a bullet. The Dodge behind us might be carrying vampires, might not. Either way, I didn't have to kill them to protect myself—and Crystal.

I could just stop them.

And if they were vampires... well, I would deal with them later.

Both hands up, I concentrated on the earth. A shaft of stone about as thick as a man's thigh sprang up—behind the truck. The Caddy swerved around it, though scraped the side, the mirror exploding in a blast of shimmery glass bits. Shit. The ground is moving by so fast, aiming at the road between us won't work. Against my instinct, I focused my—magic for lack of a better term—straight down and drew another rock spire upward.

It took a second or two to form, plenty of time for us to be away before it erupted.

The Dodge attempted to swerve but didn't have anywhere near enough time. They crashed into the column close to the passenger side, smashing that headlight. While the column broke away from the ground from the force of the collision, the truck's rear end swung out into a spin... and the Dodge careened out of sight. Two of the guys in back fell out of the bed before it went off the edge of the road... and down into the stone quarry.

A flicker of spiraling headlights illuminated the wall of the quarry canyon.

Before I could think 'aww, shit,' a loud metallic *whump* echoed up from below.

"Nice!" yelled Crystal.

"Not nice..." I sighed, staring at the Caddy's headlights, still following us. "I just killed a bunch of people."

"People who were trying to shoot you, Max. Self-defense. And they might be vampires... in which case, they're going to get back up and continue the chase on foot, perhaps."

A bloom of orange flames illuminated the quarry behind us.

"Or not," said Crystal.

"Still." I took a deep breath, held it a moment, and let it out my nose. "I've never killed anyone before."

"Wow, you're a sentimental kinda guy, aren't you?"

"Killing is wrong."

Bang! An orange flash came from the Caddy's passenger side. My truck's rear window disintegrated into a rain of little snowy bits, and a two-inch hole appeared in the windshield.

"Tell that to them!" shouted Crystal, swerving back and forth across both lanes.

At least on the straightaway, we had the luxury of *knowing* no other cars came at us from the front.

The gun went off twice more, missing both times.

"Can I suggest you throw that car into the quarry, too?"

I stared at the headlights through my missing back window. "You want me to kill them?"

"The thought has crossed my mind, yes. Or at least do *something* to get them off our ass."

If they hit another rock column dead on, it should stop them cold. But, they'd try to swerve and might go spinning into the quarry like the truck. I didn't want to risk killing them. Bah. I'd rather risk revealing myself to be something paranormal than slaughtering people, even idiots trying to kill me. Somewhere, I'd read about a thing the cops had to kill engines with an electrical jolt. Maybe I could do the same thing.

Since they'd obligingly destroyed my rear window, I pointed a hand at the front of the car chasing us. Lightning moved *much* faster than stone. Concentrate... desire...

Boom!

A thick, jagged shaft of blinding electricity connected my fingertips to the grille of the Caddy. Sparks and smoke erupted from under the hood, washing up over the windshield.

Crystal screamed in surprise at the painfully loud blast.

The Caddy's headlights went out, and the car limped to a halt. My companion slowed down and stopped as well, then glanced over at me. "Should we deal with this now or keep going?"

I took out my cell phone and started recording video of the car, hoping I'd be able to later read the license plate. "Nah. There's at least one guy in there with a gun. Keep going."

The rear driver side door flew open. A thin white-haired guy in a nice suit jumped out, raising a handgun toward us.

"Go, go, go!" I shouted, ducking.

Crystal stomped on the gas. The guy opened fire, hitting the truck a couple times, but in the tailgate, or somewhere that didn't blow out a tire or cause a gasoline fire. At the end of the straightaway, with no one in hot pursuit, Crystal slowed again to a speed that wouldn't make a cop working a radar trap spill coffee all over themselves.

Finally, I allowed myself to breathe again and sighed at the hole in the windshield. It didn't even occur to me how close I'd come to death, no... I only saw dollar signs.

Damn. That's my luck for you. Replacing the windshield and rear window, patching body damage... my truck is going to set me back more than I charged for this case. Can't exactly drive around with a giant hole in my windshield... or bullet holes everywhere. Ugh. At least Hank—the mechanic I always go to—lets me pay him when I can... which was few and far between.

To distract myself from financial misery, I tapped the phone screen and played the video. After a few repeats, I paused it on the clearest shot of the old bastard and zoomed in so his face filled the screen. Other than a strong suspicion he came from the Farrington family, I didn't recognize him. Never did understand how that happened. Those families basically owned Shadow Pines and controlled ninety percent of what went on in and around it, but almost no one outside of their circles knew what the hell they looked like.

That didn't make any sense to me. What's the point of having all that money and power if you spend every waking moment hidden away somewhere?

"Hey, you know who this guy is?" I held the phone out so she could see.

"Yeah. Nigel Farrington."

"Nigel?"

Crystal laughed. "Isn't there *always* a Nigel in those rich families?"

"Only in British sitcoms."

She giggled. Actually giggled… and it was the most adorable thing I'd ever seen.

"So, who is this guy?"

"Umm…" She bit her lip. "I think he's Bradford Farrington's brother."

I glanced at her. "Great. That tells me everything I need to know. And in case I'm not being clear, that's sarcasm."

She sighed. "Bradford is the current elder patriarch. His younger brother, Nigel, is in his sixties, but doesn't have a lot of clout within the family."

"Enough to get a truckload of guys with rifles to chase us around. Guys that I freakin' killed." I rubbed my forehead.

"You don't know that…"

I blinked at her. "They went off a forty foot cliff and blew up in a fireball."

She shrank a little. "Okay, maybe we do know that. But still… they were shooting at us."

"Right."

"And they tried to kidnap me!" She made this imploring face at me that melted away my guilt. Fairly sure she used some kind of charm power on me. Suppose being a sucker for a pretty face goes hand-in-hand with being a private detective, but even I'm not *that* bad. Wide blue eyes don't normally erase guilt over taking life. But, okay… if someone was about to shoot Crystal, I'd put a .44 in their heart without a second thought. I'd probably be messed up about it for a while afterward, maybe forever, but I couldn't let someone hurt her.

Unable to sort out how I felt about causing that crash, or, worse, how I felt about not feeling much of anything about it at all, I settled down in the seat and let Crystal drive us to Ironside.

Great. A city full of werewolves—just what we needed.

Chapter Twenty-Five
Ironside

Ironside got its name from mining.

At least, I was fairly certain it had. The town stood damn close to the mountains, and much of its economy had been based around the extraction of iron ore. About thirty miles of forest—and one tunnel where the road cut through a swath of rocky hills—separated it from Shadow Pines.

It boasted a bizarre combination of outdoorsy and industrial. The inner parts of the city felt a lot like Pittsburgh from about twenty years ago, while everywhere not 'downtown' had a vibe more like Boulder, Colorado. Some of the ironworks still operated, though with the glut of steel being imported these days, most of the smelting plants stood idle. Half the town reinvented itself as a 'go to' tourist destination for people looking for the 'outdoorsman's experience' who also didn't have much of a budget. Some even referred to Ironside as the 'poor man's Aspen.'

The town offered plenty of cheap hotels, ski lodges, hiking guides, small mom and pop coffee places, and so on. After what Crystal said about werewolves, the abundance of that 'natural' vibe here took on a new light. Conflict—of sorts—did exist between the 'rugged' types who'd been there forever and the influx of new hipster nature people. I guess the old guard thought of them as posers, acting all concerned for the environment, but doing it more to be trendy than out of any true connection to nature.

No one paid us much attention as we drove into town. We stopped at the first place I spotted that looked like it'd make for a decent, fast meal. I didn't realize they only sold vegan burgers until after we got back into the truck with our dinner. Oh well. How bad could they be? At least the fries smelled real. From there, we took a room at a tourist hotel called the Trail House Inn. The guy behind the counter really overdid the stereotype: burly dude with a beard, red flannel shirt... I couldn't help but feel like I'd stumbled into one of those movies where a town appears all innocent during the day but everyone turns into flesh-eating monsters at night.

We sat at the little table in the hotel room to eat. And, okay, the vegan burgers didn't taste bad. I'd never mistake it for real meat, but at the moment, I didn't much care. My thoughts about my damaged truck, the case, possibly having one of the Founding Families after my head, the general existence of vampires, werewolves, succubi, and actual magic all fell by the wayside. Sitting so close across the table from Crystal, I found myself uncharacteristically lost for words.

Did she style her hair like that on purpose because she thought the 'draped over one eye' thing would endear her to a private detective? I can't say I'd seen too many girls rocking a retro style like that. But it worked for her. She could totally pull off the vintage Hollywood bombshell, but more to the ingénue side than femme fatale. Looks could—and often were—deceiving. In her case, very much so. After all, I'd seen the girl throw a chunk of bannister through a vampire's chest.

And that thought jogged my brain out of the schoolboy crush haze it had been floating in ever since we sat down to eat. Crystal was a succubus, or at least a half of one. Her real father had been a creature she referred to as an incubus—which I assumed to be the male version of a succubus. Without doing any research, I had only bits and pieces of folklore I'd picked up on over the years to go by. And, some people might think that wouldn't amount to much, but if the residents of Shadow Pines had anything, it would be an abundance of folklore. Which made sense, considering this shit was all real. In hindsight, everything I grew up hearing and thinking of as 'crazy old people telling stories' was sounding more and more like serious life advice.

Well, I'd thought of succubi as demons, which may not be accurate. However, they also supposedly charmed and devoured men. (Or women in the case of Incubi). Considering that Crystal's mother remained alive, and had given birth to her, that suggested that some of those rumors of 'devouring' had been overstated. Demon or not, those thoughts didn't change my sudden doubt that the feelings she stirred inside me from first sight might not be genuine. When I'd first laid eyes on Justine—well not the *first* time. Meaning, we'd both grown up in this town, so it wasn't as if I'd never looked at her. I'd known of her for most of my life, but didn't really *see* her in that way until a few years ago. Yeah, it's shallow now that I think about it, and she's probably right to call me an asshole, but with her, things had been heavy on the lust. Something about her 'take no shit' attitude, confidence, and utter lack of fear had turned me on big time.

She claimed I 'hurt' her, but it wasn't like I cheated on her or ignored her or did anything I'd consider really bad. Part of it came from our arguing over her not thinking private investigation amounted to a 'real' job and wanting me to get something more stable. The rest of it came from me avoiding conversations whenever she brought up that whole 'long term commitment' thing. Perhaps something deep inside me knew she wasn't the 'right one' for me. Whenever she started talking about anything long term, I'd kinda zone out or change the subject. And, yeah, I guess that counted as being an asshole. I should've been straight with her.

But refer back to the lust part...

Anyway, the instant I first saw Crystal, it had been completely different. Justine, I'd wanted to get in bed as fast as possible, but not Crystal. She set off all sorts of those scary 'long term commitment' thoughts right away. I hadn't wanted to find the fastest way into the sack with her, more like I wanted to be with her in every conceivable way. Just sitting here eating vegan burgers and talking made me happier than going all the way with Justine ever did.

Yet, as I sat there munching on my fake-a-burger, I couldn't shake the nagging worry that everything I felt for her came from mental influence. It hit me like heartbreak and betrayal and terror all wrapped up into one petite little blonde package.

Crystal shifted her eyes up from her food to stare at me. "What's wrong?"

"That's kind of a silly question considering everything that's happened."

She almost smiled. "Obviously. No, I meant your mood changed so fast. Like, in the past few minutes. It's as though you just found out someone close to you died."

"You can read emotions off people?"

"Only after I've been around them for a little

while, or start to think of them fondly." She stuck a single French fry into her mouth, past an impish smile.

"Trying to sort out some things in my head."

"You finally stopped to think about what I am."

Unprepared for her directness, I tried to buy a second to think with a chuckle. "I…"

"That's sweet. You thought I've charmed you and that's where your sudden sadness came from."

In all my twenty-eight years, I could recall only blushing twice. Once in eighth grade when my little friend decided to stand at attention randomly in the middle of class and got noticed by a girl in the next row. The second time? Right now. "Something like that. *Did* you charm me? Up until you walked into my office, I never really believed in that love at first sight thing. I'm questioning if my feelings are genuine."

"What sort of feelings do you have?"

I couldn't look at her anymore. Except not making eye contact didn't do anything to help. I wasn't used to being the kind of guy who mentally shut down when encountering the pretty girl, but damned if my brain didn't turn off. I felt like the babbling idiot who couldn't string two words together when his crush finally noticed him. "Umm. This is going to sound incredibly lame, but from the minute you… um… first showed up at my office, I wanted more than anything for you to be part of… well, to be part of my life."

She tilted her head in contemplation.

"I'm sure you get plenty of guys falling over themselves, but the feelings I had were nothing like with Justine."

"How long were you with the sheriff?"

I winced. "Briefly. Things didn't work out. She had this whole list of unreasonable demands."

She raised an eyebrow. "Such as?"

"Oh, you know... wanting me to get a steady job instead of working for myself. Keep regular hours, do something with my life. You know, unreasonable."

Crystal laughed. "I know her. And I'm beginning to know you better and better. The two of you are totally incompatible."

"Yeah, found that out the hard way. With her, it was mostly just a physical thing. When I saw you, it wasn't only your body... it felt like something went way deeper."

"And, now you're wondering if I somehow did that to you on purpose." She looked down at her food, her eyes tinted with sorrow. I knew in that moment someone she'd trusted with her secret had hurt her... somehow. No, not me. Someone else.

"This is all new to me," I said. "Dealing with vampires and other things that should be myths. If you felt my emotion change, that loss—like someone died—came from the fear that how I felt toward you might not have been real. I want it to be real."

She looked up, trying to smile past whatever weight had settled on her heart. "I know. Your feelings are probably genuine, though I do give off a continuous weak charm that I can't do anything about. But it wouldn't have made you feel the way you feel. Usually, it just causes men—rather, anyone attracted to women—to trust me. It's not the same as a full-blooded succubus. They can supposedly charm men to the point that memory fails. One look, and guys just stand there dumbfounded."

I grinned. "You had that effect on me, but I remember every second of it."

Crystal laughed, her voice bright and free of sadness. "This might be a little forward of me, but would you like to have sex?"

I leaned back, blinked, and rubbed my earlobe. "Did you just ask me if I wanted to have sex?"

She folded her arms on the table, smiling. "I did. And yes, before you ask, I'm hungry... for sexual energy. It's how I feed, remember? No, it won't hurt."

"With any other woman I'd ever dated, even before I knew them well, I'd be halfway to the bed already, cheering. But... are you sure? We've only known each other for a few days. Feels almost like I'm taking advantage of you."

Crystal stood and offered a hand. "I know what I look like. Don't feel that way. If anyone's taking advantage here, it's me."

Who was I to say no to that? I still felt a bit like whatever we had would be cheapened by casual sex so soon, but I also appreciated my hypocrisy considering how things had been with Justine. That said, Crystal and I soon wound up on the bed together, no clothes between us, holding each other. Something definitely worked differently with this girl… every time we kissed, a tingle sparked at my lips and rushed down inside me to parts unknown, and bounced back up.

Oh, yeah… I was about to have one hell of a night…

Chapter Twenty-Six
Worth It. Definitely Worth It.

I felt like a juice box that had been sucked on until it imploded.

My body had gone numb from the waist down except for the important parts, which admittedly, kind of ached. It wasn't the 'kicked in the balls an hour ago' sort of ache that I loathed, though it came close. However, if she wanted to do that again, I wouldn't hesitate at all. We'd just shared the most amazing almost-hour of my life… even if I did feel as though I'd been run over by a bus. She'd certainly drained quite a bit of energy out of me—through a rather specific part of my anatomy.

Crystal lay on her side nearby, gently stroking her fingers around my chest. I appreciated not being alone. If a vampire kicked in the door right now, I'd probably be dead. Ever have an alarm clock go off after three hours of sleep and have one of those mornings where you'd rather find a new job than get out of bed? Yeah, that times ten is where I found myself. If the Farringtons sent some thugs after us here, I could see myself just lying still and not caring what they did to us.

For her part, she seemed energized and put on this contagiously happy grin. I would've been grinning too if I had the strength left to move my lips. Somewhere between fatigue and that 'holy shit that was awesome' feeling like it had been my very first time with a girl, I couldn't be bothered to do anything but stare at the ceiling. In fact, I'm not sure my body *would* move if I tried.

"Are you sure you want to be involved with me?" asked Crystal in a partial whisper.

Was she seriously questioning if I'd never want to experience that again? "Absolutely. You're the most incredible woman I've ever met... in every conceivable way."

She smiled, and cuddled closer, resting her cheek on my chest. "You aren't worried it might not work out between us long term? Whoever heard of an elementalist and a succubus together?"

I raised an eyebrow. "Whoever heard of an elementalist at all?"

Crystal giggled. "True. Well, we could see where this goes. Are you all right? I didn't take too much, did I?"

"I wasn't expecting that... but I'm fine. More than fine. Amazing even."

"Your energy felt so different from the others. I've never had anyone seriously in love with me before."

Of course, she referred to it as 'feeding,' which meant sex. I hated thinking about how many men she'd probably been with, but resisted the notion of her being a 'loose woman.' Nature compelled her to engage in sex for nutritional sake. If she didn't do it, she'd starve to death. Human morals probably shouldn't apply to non-humans. Or even half humans. And really, who decided that men can bed dozens of women and that's something to brag about, but it works the opposite way for women? That is kinda messed up.

"So, umm... how long before I can move?" I asked.

She laughed again, perhaps thinking I joked about not being able to move. "You should be all right by morning."

"That's good to know."

"Most succubi don't do long-term relationships well. One guy is sometimes not enough to feed me. For a *full* succubus? It wouldn't even approach possible. The poor guy would wither away if she tried to sustain herself exclusively from one person."

"Ouch. So what you're saying is, you're going to need other men?"

She stroked her hand over my chest in front of her face. "It depends on how rough things get. The more often I use supernatural abilities, the faster I get hungry in *that* way. If the poo really hits the fan, I'd need to consume more than you could safely give. I still need to eat real food, too. True succubi don't. And, they also leave a guy out of sorts for a few days afterward."

"How do you know so much about them?"

"My real father visited me a few times after the family exiled me to Ironside. He filled in all the missing pieces that explained so much about my crazy life. I'm not sure what surprises me more, that I actually told you the truth about me, or that I feel drawn to you as well. Maybe we *could* make it work… if you can handle that I might sometimes need to sustain myself by feeding from someone else."

"Would it bother you if I tolerated it but didn't like it?"

"It wouldn't have any deeper meaning to me than eating dinner."

I wanted to curl my arm around her, but couldn't move it. "That's why I'd tolerate it. It's just something you have to do, like food, water, air…"

"If you're the jealous type, I could try to feed on women instead."

I coughed.

"Yes, that's possible, but it's more difficult. I can't charm a woman unless she's gay, and that kinda reduces the size of the buffet. I can feed from guys and have them not even remember anything that happened if I want to… well, unless they're into men."

"I guess making them forget is best. Won't break anyone's heart that way." I sighed mentally. Except possibly mine. Just gotta keep thinking about it being food to her. Wow, my life has gone *way* off the rails.

"Is there any truth to the stories of succubi killing men?"

"Maybe full-blooded succubi. We feed on sexual energy and life essence, and they consume a lot more than I do. If they take too much from one person, their energy won't regenerate... and it could either kill them or leave them a hollow, lifeless shell incapable of embracing life or feeling the slightest bit of joy or enthusiasm."

"You might have just described Cleveland Browns fans everywhere."

"A sports team?"

"Yes, although their luck might have changed recently."

"It always does, don't you know?"

"I'm beginning to believe it. So, um, how often do you need to... feed?"

"If I behave myself and don't use any of my powers, then about once a week. A human physically recovers from my feeding in about six hours, but it takes them about seven-to-ten days to spiritually recover."

"So, once a week is pushing it."

"It is... and I'm kinda bad at behaving myself. I like my powers and use them often." She leaned up and kissed me. "But, I'm not used to a man who is willing to feed me *and* has fallen in love with me. The energy is stronger, so maybe I won't actually have to feed as often."

"Guess I'm high calorie."

"Maybe. I never really thought about that. I've mostly been feeding as discreetly as possible ever since I became old enough to have that need."

"Are you like 300 years old or something?"

"No. I'm twenty-six. My actual father did say we live longer than normal people, but he didn't really offer much detail. Full-blooded succubi and incubi are immortal. Do I look younger than twenty-six to you?"

"A little. Not much. I'd have guessed maybe twenty-two."

"Thank you." She kissed me again. "Well, we still do have the problem of Nigel Farrington wanting to abduct me… and possibly wanting you out of the way."

I said, "Yeah, yeah," in my best 'it can wait for effing tomorrow' tone.

"The severity of the problem would depend on if those vampires belonged to Farrington's circle or if it had been a momentary arrangement to deal with me."

I processed this. At least my brain still worked, foggy as it was. "Somehow, your sister Dana discovered that he intended to attack you, but the vampires killed her before she could warn you. Something bothers me about that."

"Only 'bothers' you?"

"I don't mean her death. Forgive me for not sitting up. I still can't really move."

"It's all right. I prefer using you as a pillow."

I chuckled. "What bothers me is if Dana found out this information, why did she go to a party out in the forest? Why not call you right away with a warning and give you all the details? Unless she went to that party specifically to find out more information. You did tell me it had weird occult overtones."

"Hmm. That's true. What do you think happened?"

"I'm guessing here, but try this idea on for size. The Farringtons somehow find out that you're a succubus. Or maybe it's Nigel working independently. He can't get to you in Ironside, so he needs to do something that will bring you within reach. You're at odds with your family, so he doesn't think they'll get in his way."

"More than 'at odds.' My pretend father disowned me. Only my mother and Dana cared to have anything to do with me. Mother, at least, put me back into the will after his passing. And no, I had nothing to do with his death."

It happened two years ago. I'd heard about it... the whole town had. "Did a bear really swim all the way out to his fishing boat?"

"No one really believes a bear did it."

"Well, I used to... up to a few days ago. I figured if a cub wound up on that boat, a mama bear would have gone after it... but, knowing what I know

now…"

"Right."

"Any idea who killed him or why?"

"I have my suspicions."

"Care to share them?"

"I figure vampires allied with the Anworth family killed him. It'll never be proven though. No one's looking for the truth. Few people would believe the truth if it came out, and there isn't a single person involved who'd want it out in the open."

"What makes you think the Anworths did it?"

She lay there in silence for a while.

"That bad, huh? Okay. I won't push."

Crystal sighed. "It's a bit sensitive, but I've already told you about me, so I'll trust you with one more secret. But, you must give me your word you won't speak of it to anyone."

I stared down the length of her perfect body, pressed to my side like one of those artsy nude photos that didn't show any naughty bits. Not that I could've moved if I wanted to, but of anywhere on Earth I could've been, I wouldn't have changed a thing. "Keeping secrets is what I do for a living."

"Isn't it your job to *expose* secrets?"

"True, but secrets I've been asked to keep are another thing."

"All right." She lowered her voice to a whisper. "My pseudo-father was having an affair with Brittany Anworth."

"And her husband wanted revenge?"

"No. She's not married. The woman's only a year older than me."

I winced. "So he was seeing a girl young enough to be his daughter?"

"Yes, but that isn't what caused the problem. The Bradburys and Anworths have been at each other's throats for 200 years. We've hated each other for so long I don't think anyone remembers what started it. Before this part of the country had a well-developed police force, random murders and even small armed skirmishes between groups of twenty or so men per side happened all the time. It's the only time I can ever say anything good about chauvinism."

"No killing women or children?"

"Basically."

"Sounds like your old man got over the feud... as did that girl... Brittany."

"He's not really my father. But, I suspect they fell in love. Somehow, the rest of her family found out and wanted to put a stop to it."

My arm finally decided to listen to me again, so I reached up and rested it on her back. "So you don't think the attack on Dana had anything to do with the Anworth situation?"

"No. The Farringtons wouldn't have cared at all who Sterling Bradbury slept with. I'm sure Nigel had his vampires target Dana in hopes I'd return to Shadow Pines for the funeral... which I did."

"Wait. You live here in Ironside."

"I do."

"Then why are we in a hotel?"

She laughed. "Well, you were driving and you got the wild idea. My place is tiny, and a mess, and at the time I hadn't planned on us winding up in bed together. We can relocate in the morning if you like."

"Hmm. I'd prefer getting Nigel off your back first. How do you feel about returning to Shadow Pines once the sun's up? Maybe you can go invisible and snoop around Justine's office. She might have information she hasn't shared. While you're doing that, I'll rattle a few other trees and see what I can find."

"All right. Sounds like a reasonable plan. Oh darn. I left my car by the quarry. Think it will still be there in the morning?"

"Probably. Something tells me Nigel isn't going to want to draw attention to why he was out there. And it'll take a couple days before anyone notices a truck went off the side. Maybe even long enough for them to sweep the mess under the proverbial rug."

Crystal pulled the sheets and blanket up to cover us, and closed her eyes. "Good night, Max."

The past few days had seen quite a few moments where I expected to wake up from a dream beyond belief.

Falling asleep next to a woman as perfect as Crystal Bradbury was one of them.

Chapter Twenty-Seven
A Search for Understanding

I paced around my apartment, alternating between worried and grinning at Crystal's clothes on my bed.

We'd left the hotel a little after eight, stopped by her place so she could change, then headed back to Shadow Pines with a detour to recover her car. My place didn't have much in the sense of real food, so we also grabbed breakfast from a place across the street and down a block.

She'd walked out the door a few minutes ago with only her invisibility on; hence, the clothing on my bed. Fortunately, the sheriff's office wasn't too far away, a little over a mile. That could prove to be a problem if the vampires or whoever is pulling Justine's strings spotted her. I could only hope she made it there without detection. After all, she certainly appeared invisible to me... and killer vamps should be snoozing about now.

While Crystal headed to check out the sheriff's office, I called Michael. At present, I could count the number of sources available to get 'weird' information on one hand. Presently, that amounted to two. Michael and Crystal. She obviously had no idea why the Farringtons wanted her, other than presumably her being a succubus, so I had one person left to ask.

"Hey, Max. Good to hear you're still alive," said Michael by way of answering.

"For the time being… You were right. Only they didn't come after me. I went after them."

"Great. I'm guessing it ended well since you're on the phone with me, unless this is a direct line from the hereafter."

I chuckled and sat in the chair by my computer desk. Well, it's technically a folding card table, but it's my computer station. While sipping the last of the coffee I'd gotten from Benny's place, I gave Michael a quick rundown of what happened at the old boarding house. For her privacy, I left out that Crystal had accompanied me or that she was anything other than human.

"Holy shit. I kinda heard about that."

"You did?" I asked, incredulous. "How?"

"Those college kids you found were on the news this morning. They'd been missing a couple days, same old story—hiking and presumed lost."

"Ugh. If I had a buck for every time that happened in Shadow Pines. Most people around here translate that to 'never to be seen again.'"

"Right. Only, these kids came back. Claimed they'd been abducted by a couple of crazy hermits or something who'd been squatting in the abandoned boarding house. No mention of vampires, unsurprisingly, but they did wind up in the hospital for 'observation.'"

Oops. Crystal and I never did go back for them. Guess they managed to get out of that room. I can picture that redhead, Shiloh, breaking the door down. And I had, after all, given her the key to that BMW. Bigger question is if they decided not to talk about vampires on their own, or if someone made sure they didn't. Considering they haven't disappeared again, I assumed they decided to keep their mouths shut.

I shook my head. "You'd have to think the doctors would start to suspect something weird was going on around here with all the cases of people being 'low on blood'."

Michael laughed. "They probably do... and are made to forget once they ask too many questions."

"Speaking of questions, I got one for you."

"Shoot."

"Shit. You just reminded me I need to drop the truck off at Hank's. Anyway... do you have any idea why someone would want to capture a half-succubus?"

"Umm, only that they're an idiot. Those critters are pretty much impossible to contain. Also, supposedly quite dangerous. I've heard of a few reports, but the information is somewhat sketchy. They might be demons, might be something else."

"Fey."

"That's one theory, yeah. I'd recommend you stay the heck away from them."

I shifted in the seat, stifling a grunt at the soreness in my groin. "Let's say in theory someone managed to find a way to contain one with, oh, a strange green energy field."

"You saw this?"

"The barrier felt like glass, kinda looked like green lasers in smoke. It was round, and came up from a circle drawn on the floor."

"And it worked? Someone actually captured a succubus?"

"Yeah. Half-succubus, not a full one. What would they want her for?"

Rustling crackled over the line, as though he held the phone to his head with his shoulder while rummaging books or binders. "Gimme a sec."

"Sure."

I glanced across the room past the bedroom door at her clothes on the bed. Sneaking into a police station is probably one of the dumbest things a person can do. Doing it naked is next level. Though, she *is* invisible, can open any lock she touches, and/or can teleport short distances. So, yeah, Michael's right… containing a succubus with physical means is pretty much futile.

"Hmm," said Michael after a few minutes of

paper shuffling. "Someone capable of creating the barrier you're describing might be interested in her essence."

"Her essence?"

"Yeah, like her soul energy or whatever. As you might expect, taking that from her would be fatal... to her, of course." He rummaged some more while I waited. Truth was, I was still damn weak, but at least I could move now. Michael came back on the line five, ten minutes later. "Okay. Best I can figure, they're looking to create a magical artifact with the ability to control minds. Succubus essence could also be used for an invisibility item—but then again any fey spirit can—or this one I'm reading about here sounds like a continuous radiant charm. Like, if they put it into a ring or bit of jewelry, whoever wore the item would be so charismatic everyone around them would think they're the greatest thing since sliced bread. No matter *what* they did, people would love them. Barring, of course, anyone immune or resistant to charm."

Damn. That sounds bad. I can't let that happen. "Is there any way to protect her?"

"Protect her? You know the succubus?"

"We've... met."

Michael kept silent.

A half-minute passed. "Michael?"

"You did it, didn't you?"

I sighed. "Any possible way I respond to that you're going to take as an admission that something happened."

"Something happened."

"See?"

He whistled. "Max, you could help me out with some information. I don't have a lot here on succubi. No need to reveal who she is, but any concrete facts you can share would be amazingly helpful."

"I'll ask. She's kinda private. But I will say they're definitely fey and not demons. Nor do they kill. They're not inherently dangerous. Bear in mind, I'm talking about a half-succubus here. No idea what the purebloods are like. So… what's the best way to make sure the bad guys don't keep going after her?"

Michael murmured as if jotting down notes for a few seconds. "Best way? Either kill the person or persons trying to take her power, or kill her."

I grumbled.

"I realize that's not a wonderful answer, but it *is* the best way to guarantee that the artifact is never created. I suppose you could attempt to talk the arcanist out of it, but I don't imagine that would work too well. If they've already gone to the trouble of creating an entrapment field, they're committed."

"Arcanist?"

"Would it be easier for you to understand if I called them a wizard?"

"Easier to understand, yes. Believe? Not so much."

"You throw lightning bolts from your hands, Max. I've seen it."

I rubbed my face, groaning.

216

"An arcanist is similar but different. You *are* nature. The power is both around you and inside you. Using it is as natural as breathing or walking. Arcanists manipulate forces comparable to yours, though it is completely external. For them, it takes years of focus and study, memorizing specific thought patterns, hand motions, runes, that sort of thing. Most of what they do needs to be channeled into the form of items or, like that circle, inscribed on the floor, walls, paper, and so on. They are also quite rare. A person needs to be born with the ability to invoke magic, but if they never pursue it, it will never develop. In the modern world where the collective consciousness of humanity largely regards things like magic as mythological, the vast majority of those who have the propensity to become arcanists never realize it."

"Well, that's too bad for them… but at least one guy around here figured it out. Maybe more than one. I really don't know."

"If you wind up having to deal with him or them directly, you should have the advantage. They would be reliant on trinkets and traps."

A sudden feeling of no longer being alone came over me. I sat up and looked around, stretching my arm to grab the .44 beside the computer keyboard. Learning that vampires really existed didn't worry me as much as learning the sun didn't destroy them. Sure, they're weaker in daylight, but a highly motivated vampire wouldn't let that stop them. And killing an entire pack is plenty enough to motivate their friends.

But… I didn't invite anyone inside. Thank God for that crazy rule.

With that thought in mind, I shifted my attention to the window, scanning the buildings across the street for someone watching me with binoculars. Something moved in the corner of my eye. I whirled to my left, aiming my gun at… Crystal's underwear floating up off the bed. Oh, for the love of…

The flying panties stretched out, sank down near the floor, then took on the shape of the woman pulling them up into place.

"So, there's nothing 'magical' that can be done to protect her?" I asked, spinning away and setting the .44 down on the table.

"Afraid not."

"Damn. Hey, I need to go, Michael. Give me a call if you find something?"

"Will do. Be careful, Max."

"I'd say I will, but you wouldn't believe me."

He laughed.

Crystal walked out of the bedroom as I set the phone down. She didn't look too happy, but she also didn't look angry.

"I'm guessing you didn't find anything useful," I said.

"More or less. I couldn't get into her computer, but her desk drawers and file cabinets had some stuff that makes me think she's in bed with the Blackwood family. Couldn't tell if she's been influenced with supernatural means or the old fashioned way. I'd assumed the Farringtons had her, but I think I guessed wrong."

"Bribes? I don't see Justine taking bribes."

"Might not be money. Could be threats, or merely an appeal that she maintain the appearance that nothing strange goes on here. She definitely knew more about Dana and Luke's murder than she's told anyone, including you. Trust me. But, I didn't see anything that implied she acted at the direction of the Farringtons." She sighed and fell seated on the couch. "My best guess is that she probably just wanted to keep my sister's murder quiet because vampires had been involved."

I leaned back in my chair, folding my arms. "Damn. That doesn't help us with the Nigel problem—that is, if he's our main problem—but at least it's a good sign that we won't have to worry about Justine or the cops being a threat. I've got a reasonably clear video of Nigel shooting at us. Maybe we could take that to Justine and the police? Sure, the Farringtons have loads of money and influence, but even they shouldn't be able to get away with trying to murder us in the middle of the road."

"The video doesn't prove *why* he was shooting or even who he fired at. He could've been defending himself from someone who attacked him, or shooting at one of those supposed large cats prowling around."

"Why would someone in a car stop, get out, and pull a handgun on a mountain lion? They'd just keep driving."

She raised her hands. "Hey, don't bite my head off. I'm only saying what *they* will say. It's a weak story but more plausible than vampires and they'd never admit to attempting to kidnap me, succubus or not."

"Oh, I got some bad news."

"How bad?"

"Bad."

"Lemme guess... that phone call you were on when I came in."

"Good guess." I filled her in on what Michael told me regarding the reasons Nigel would want to abduct her. "He inferred that I'd met a succubus and he wanted more information. I figured you wouldn't be too interested, so I gave him some generic stuff —good PR basically."

She nodded. "I trust you to use good judgment."

We sat there in silence for a moment, looking at each other. I tapped my fingers on my makeshift desk. "I'd rather not kill Nigel... or anyone else who isn't already dead."

"Yeah." She played with her hair, twisting it around her finger, dropping it, and doing it again. "It wouldn't really bother me that much if some-thing happened to him, but I don't think we should go kill him. What if we found dirt on him, then did one of those 'if anything happens to me, it gets automatically mailed to all the news outlets' things?"

"That's technically extortion, isn't it?"

Crystal shrugged. "Not quite. We're not threatening to reveal sensitive information unless he pays us money. As long as he doesn't kidnap and murder me, he's safe. Besides, for him to go to the police about any extortion claim, he'd have to admit he intended to kidnap and murder me."

"Hmm. That might work. Any idea what he might be involved with where I could start looking?"

"You're not going to like it." She flashed a cheesy smile. "The best sources of dirt on such people are the other Founding Families. They keep track of each other like the CIA. I bet most of them even know what I am. I suppose we could try talking to my family to start out with, but they haven't been on speaking terms with me in a while... except my mother and Dana, and..." She bowed her head, close to tears.

I hurried over to sit beside her on the couch and put an arm around her. "They might have their issues with you," I said, "but they would be more upset over your sister, right? It's most likely true that the Farringtons sent those vampires after her specifically to lure you here. Wouldn't the Bradburys want to retaliate?"

She sniffled, wiped her eyes, then lifted her head to give me this heart-melting stare. How a girl like her—who is pretty damn dangerous—could look *so* timid and helpless, I had no damn idea. If she'd asked me in that moment to light myself on fire and jump out the window, I probably would've done it.

"Yeah. It's worth a try at least." She fanned herself, taking deep breaths. "I'll need to go back to my place for a more lady-like outfit. Do you have anything nice to wear?"

"Ehh, only the suit I usually wear to court, weddings, or funerals."

She blinked. "You have *one* suit?"

"Yeah, but it's at least in good shape."

"All right. I suppose we can try."

I stood. "Great. What's the worst that could happen?"

"We end up dead in a shallow grave."

"Please tell me you're exaggerating?"

She smiled and rose to her feet. "You said the worst thing. It's not likely, but it's possible."

I nearly called her a smartass, but she was right. How close to death had we been in the past few days? Too damn close.

"I'll drive," she said.

"Seeing as how my truck barely has windows? Good call."

Crystal rubbed my arm. "Sorry. I feel bad about that. At least let me cover the repairs?"

Half of my brain tried to refuse, feeling guilty for taking money from an innocent girl presently being hunted for her soul. The other half called me a moron. I wound up staring at her, unable to formulate a reply.

"It's fine. My family might have sent me packing, but Mother made sure I didn't have to worry too much about money. It's one reason I live in such a small apartment. Saving. I don't plan to spend the rest of my life in Ironside. I only need to outlive my bitchy grandmother."

"She the problem?"

"With Sterling dead, yes."

"You call your father by his first name?"

She poked me in the side and started for the door. "He wasn't my father."

Chapter Twenty-Eight
We Could Always Try Diplomacy

Under protest, I changed into my suit before we left.

Not that I had any problem with dressing nice when the situation demanded it, but if anything happened to this suit, I'd need to replace it. Maybe for some people, dropping $500 on a new suit isn't a big deal… but I use it so rarely, it's hard to justify the expense. I got it four years ago when one of my cases intersected a murder investigation. I wound up having to show up in court to testify about pictures I'd taken. One would think a cheating spouse investigation wouldn't end up in the courtroom for a murder trial, but I had a front row seat to an unfaithful husband and someone else's wife having some lakeside fun at night… and the mistress' husband showed up with murder in his eyes and—

of all things—a samurai sword.

The attack had been too sudden for me to do much about the poor bastard I'd been hired to tail, but I did stop the guy from killing his wife, too. Nothing quite like a .44 magnum to make a dude rearrange his priorities. But, yeah, courtroom, two weddings of my high school friends, and three funerals have been the extent of the need I've had to wear a suit.

I tried to make the argument that wearing a $500 suit to the Bradbury mansion would probably be *more* insulting than my usual blue button down and jeans. Something about them having more respect for my not even trying than showing up in a cheap off-the-rack thing from one of those chain menswear stores. But, she insisted... and emerged from the bedroom of her apartment in a shoulder-baring dark blue dress that sparkled whenever the light hit it just right. It bared quite a bit of her back as well, a thin crisscross of cording holding it together.

"Wow..." I blinked a few times.

"Something in your eyes?"

"No, just making sure I'm not hallucinating a goddess or something."

A hint of blush reddened her face. "Please don't say anything that embarrassingly cheesy in front of my family. They don't think of me as fondly."

"Cheesy?" I put a hand over my heart. "You wound me."

"It kinda was, but I thought it cute."

I fake wiped sweat from my brow, then held out my arm. "Shall we?"

She rolled her eyes, but took my arm. "You've not had a single bit of experience dealing with the upper class, have you?"

"Is it that obvious?"

"Yeah." She winked. "Just let me do the talking."

***

Crystal had a nice little Lexus, designed more for sport than luxury.

The car suited her well, a lot of power in a compact package, cute, dangerous, and sleek. It could've done with a bit more legroom, but I'm used to my truck. She didn't seem the type to go for the big ol' luxury land yacht type cars anyway. I got the feeling she lacked the patience for the stuffiness of the Founding Families and rather enjoyed being mostly free of it.

Most of the old money in Shadow Pines lived in the northeast part of town, where sprawling land-scapes surrounded mansions. Three of the families built their estates past the outskirts, no doubt to keep their distance from rival families. Like the Anworth estate... two miles south of town.

We drove past the downtown district, on high alert verging on paranoia, but no one attacked us or even gave us strange looks. I'm guessing the vampires tended to stay out of the sun whenever possible, especially this early in the day. Assuming they had to sleep at all, it stood to reason they probably would have been out cold after staying up all night. Crystal drove through a few residential areas and took a pastoral road with brand new paving and storybook-perfect trees on both sides. We passed two private driveways about four minutes apart. She turned left into the third one. I wondered if having an estate where you can see your neighbor's house made it a 'McMansion.' The Anworth estate I'd been to once, if following a suspected cheating husband and waiting outside the gate for him to do cable TV work inside counts as 'been to." Anyway, those people had a crapload of land. They couldn't even see the town from their windows much less another mansion.

Crystal pulled to a stop at the large gate blocking the entrance to a courtyard with a fountain at its center. A droll-faced man with salt and pepper hair in his later forties appeared via a small screen on a post-mounted console. He didn't even need to say 'what are *you* doing here?' His expression already did that.

"Hello, Pierce," said Crystal. "I know I'm not welcome, but it's important I speak to Grandmother. It's about Dana."

"There's nothing you can do for her now. The poor, misguided soul."

The screen went dark.

Crystal reached out and pushed the button. She waited a moment, then pushed it again—holding it down.

A flustered Pierce reappeared. "Must you?"

"We both know I could walk right in if I wanted to. I am attempting to be civil about this. Whatever the family thinks of me, they at least owe it to Dana to hear what I have to say regarding the reasons she was killed. If you don't at least tell Grandmother I wish to speak to her, I'll do so myself."

Pierce sneered at her the way I'd expect her deceased stepfather, the former mayor, to look down at a homeless guy who'd touched his suit. Then again, I'm not sure where that thought came from. "Very well. One moment."

The screen went dark again.

"I sincerely want to punch that man." I looked at my hands. "Or turn his dick to stone."

She giggled and leaned back into her seat, facing forward. "So do I. The punching him part, I mean." Crystal turned her head to look at me. "Something against the wealthy, or that man in particular?"

"Although I can't say I've got a lot of love for the snob crowd, there's no animosity on my end. No, that guy in particular—for looking down at you like that."

"He looks down on everyone who isn't one of the Families, and looks down worse on anyone who *was* one of the Families."

"That doesn't make me want to slug him any less."

We sat there for a few minutes. Crystal mostly

told me random stories of her childhood. Dana had been two years older than her, and they'd been close as children, remaining so even after the 'exile.' Her sister's fondness caused a bit of a row with the family, but not so much they gave her the boot as well. Marrying a man from outside one of the families bothered them more. Luke Hayden, an attorney, hadn't been poor by any means, though he didn't come from 'old money.' She started telling me about how her sister had met the handsome lawyer from LA and fallen immediately in love with him, when Pierce appeared once more on the little monitor.

"Mrs. Bradbury has agreed to give you a few minutes of her time on the condition you remove yourself from the premises the instant she requests you to do so."

"That's fine," said Crystal in a tone that changed the meaning to 'eat a dick.'

He either ignored it or missed it, nodded, and disappeared. A second after the screen went dark, the large iron gate in front of us motored inward, the end rolling on a fat little tire like the kind you see on a riding lawn mower.

Crystal drove in, circled the fountain, and pulled into one of five parking spaces labeled 'visitor' on the left side. She didn't say anything, but her short, harsh motions turning off the ignition and getting out told me she hated feeling like a 'visitor' at her childhood home. Whatever animosity existed between her and Grandmother Bradbury didn't appear to be enough to get over her attachment to this old place. Spend enough years as a child somewhere and it's forever 'home.'

Her high heels (dark blue like the dress) clicked over the pavement. I put on my best attempt at a high society bearing and followed. Hey, I'd seen Titanic. I'm hardly Jack Dawson, but I can fake it. Maybe.

We stepped up onto an enormous porch with ivy-enshrouded columns, fancy brickwork and old wicker furniture. The place looked like a cross between Dracula's estate and one of those creepy ass British manor houses from like *Flowers in the Attic*. This place had secrets, I had no doubt—and most of them probably ran on the ugly side. Tall multi-panel windows looked in on a sitting room decorated in dark colors as well as an entry foyer.

A brown-haired woman in a black polo shirt and leggings—no doubt a servant of some form—appeared in the distance and hurried over to the door with an expression that made her look like she did something she expected to get in trouble for. The woman opened the door for us and backed out of the way. Crystal offered a friendly nod to her, then looked around at the foyer as well as a giant chandelier above us. I expected a wistful sigh of longing, but her expression hardened to one of rebellious defiance. Maybe I misjudged her and she didn't really miss the place. Being here might make her think about Dana's death.

The woman wordlessly led us down the hall,

into a hallway on the left, and to a set of dark mahogany double doors. She opened those and stepped inside, waiting for us to enter before closing them behind us.

I felt like we'd walked into the set of an old movie. With the exception of there being electric lights on the walls, the décor gave off an early 1900s vibe. An older woman with dark pewter-grey hair sat in a wingback chair on the left side of the room. Her dress, similar in color to Crystal's, appeared plainer, though probably still cost a ridiculous amount. I'd guess her age around seventy, though she had a severe presence that made me feel somewhat like we'd been sent to the principal's office.

Grandma Bradbury, of course.

Chapter Twenty-Nine
Darth Grandma

Crystal approached her grandmother, standing a short distance in front of her as though she'd come to seek an audience with a queen.

"This better be good," said the elder Bradbury.

I walked over to stand next to Crystal. Since she didn't sit, I made no move to either.

The grandmother gave me the most casual of glances as if noting me a servant brought along for whatever purpose.

"Nigel Farrington is the reason Dana was killed."

A small crack appeared in the old woman's absolute lack of interest in being near Crystal. Her expression softened almost imperceptibly, eyebrows easing back from their furrow. "I trust you have something more than an accusation?"

"We do, but it's not the sort of thing that would sway the police, nor would I be foolish enough to take it to them. Nigel sent two of his vampires to kill her knowing it would lure me back here from Ironside."

Slight dimples formed on either side of Grandmother's mouth, the most minimal of unimpressed smirks. "And why do you think you are significant enough for such a plot?"

Something about having the power of the elements at my disposal, daydreaming about this old bat's reaction to me ripping down this whole house —or at least doing a ton of damage to it—allowed me to keep on a pleasant face. All this wealth and fanciness didn't mean a damn thing to nature. In fact, the place stank of death. Not in the same way that coming within breathing range of a vampire did, but I didn't doubt such creatures had been here, and often. Mayor Bradbury hadn't been one, but I had started wondering if referring to politicians as bloodsuckers might be more than metaphorical around here.

"The man is an arcanist," said Crystal. "He wants to take my essence and use it to empower some sort of artifact. They almost succeeded in abducting me." She held her hand out toward me. "We have video of him personally trying to kill us."

I handed over my phone. Crystal played it, holding the phone up so the old woman could see.

"That is indeed Nigel. He seems rather perturbed," said the grandmother. "Why are you pestering me with any of this?"

"He's going to continue pursuing me until one of us is dead. I'd hoped you might have some leverage you could exploit to encourage him to forget about me."

The old one nearly laughed. "Dana is already lost. Why would I even begin to consider acting on *your* behalf after what you've done?"

Crystal shivered, though I couldn't quite tell if it came from rage, sadness, or fear.

"There's also the matter of what this guy wants to do with it," I said.

Grandmother looked up at me as astonished as if she'd witnessed a gorilla speak.

"He's going to do one of three things with her essence: craft an item that allows him to control people's minds or, create something that allows a person to become invisible. Or, worse—and probably the one he's thinking of—create a ring or amulet that gives him irresistible charm. No matter what he does, anyone in his presence would find him wonderful and do whatever he asked of them. Now, I'm no genius here, but who do you think this guy is going to turn such an item against? Normal people?" I shook my head. "He's going to use it to shift the balance of power among the families. If you won't act to protect your granddaughter, at least act out of self-interest."

"She is most certainly *not* my granddaughter," said the old woman.

A tall curtain to the left moved, revealing a man

in his young twenties wearing a beige sweater, khakis, and dock shoes. His neat brown hair looked so full of gel it would've stopped a bullet. However, unlike the old one here, he didn't regard Crystal with hostility. "Grandmother, Dana loved Crystal like a sister even after Father cast her out. Dana's dead because she wanted to protect her family."

"Arthur!" said the old one in a raised voice. "What are you doing? You know better to be in a room with... *her*. You know what will happen."

Crystal shook her head. "I do *not* charm people in my family."

The old woman scoffed.

I looked the young man over. Wow. Arthur Bradbury had been the twelve-year-old son that Sterling slapped all those years ago, back when the man had been mayor. I'd seen the pictures in the paper and on the Internet... the "Slap Heard Round the World." Shit, I feel old now.

"I suppose there's no making you hate me more than you already do. What your son told you was an absolute lie. The blonde girl that Mother caught him with was Brittany Anworth... not me."

The old woman and Arthur gasped at the same time.

"Anworth?" blurted the old one.

Crystal looked up, making eye contact with her. "I'm not sure how to react to your being more horrified at the accusation he had an affair with an Anworth rather than believing I had seduced a man pretending to be my father when I was eighteen."

It took the woman a few seconds to calm down enough to speak. "I-I find that difficult to believe. Why didn't you ever say anything before?"

"For Mother. I didn't want her to endure the grief of knowing he willingly betrayed her, especially with a girl young enough to be his daughter. If she believed that my nature compelled him against his will, she would neither blame him for it nor become angry with me. A wild dog, after all, cannot resist raw meat dangled in its face."

Arthur covered his mouth with a hand, staring at Crystal with an 'I'm so sorry' expression.

"Touching," said Grandmother with a dismissive smirk. "You could still easily be lying. Sterling is dead, so he isn't here to defend himself."

Crystal locked gazes with him. "Wide angle picture from his funeral. Third row back, fifth person in from the left."

After a momentary awkward silence, Arthur ran off, disappearing out another set of double doors.

Grandmother narrowed her eyes, though I got the feeling she suspected Crystal told the truth despite not wanting to believe her ears. No woman likes to hear that her son cheated on his wife, especially with a girl much younger than him, though that's still much less horrible than cheating with his stepdaughter. Crystal had said she and Brittany were about a year apart in age, which… ugh. Old Money had its sins, that's for damn sure. I'm guessing that woman had been around nineteen at the time, Crystal seventeen or eighteen, but took the blame to protect her mother's marriage.

Arthur returned after about ten minutes, carrying a large, framed picture. Wow... who keeps a picture of the attendees at a funeral at all, much less hangs it. The photo showed five rows of people all dressed in black standing in what I assumed to either be another sitting room of the mansion or a funeral home. Arthur traced his finger along the third row and tapped a black-haired young woman wearing a veil.

"Grandmother... she's right. That's Brittany Anworth in a black wig." He tilted the frame so she could see.

"Why else would that girl be at the funeral?" asked Crystal. "And crying. They were... much more discreet after I was 'sent away for everyone's protection.' I am not incapable of controlling myself. I can rein it in, so to speak." She paused, leveled her stare at her one-time grandma. "No, I did not seduce or feed from your son, or any other male in this family, nor would I want to."

"But Father led us to believe you had tried to seduce him..." Arthur cringed. "Why would you let us all think that of you?"

"Mother fell victim to my actual father," said Crystal. "That is to say, the male version of what I am. In his case, he was called an incubus. Mother didn't want to feed him, nor did she even remember it happened until I was born. It was less painful to let her think I had no control of a 'monster' inside me than the man she loved so much had betrayed her for another woman of his own choosing. Really, it's as simple as that."

Grandmother fidgeted. Her eyes furrowed and relaxed a few times before she took on a visage of confused defeat. "You let us think the worst of you for eleven years…"

"For Mother's benefit. I'm sorry your son wasn't what she thought."

"Oh, Sterling was no angel." Grandmother frowned. "Far from it. I should have suspected something of the sort the way he ignored your mother over the past few years."

"Grandmother… it isn't right. Father never should have disowned Crystal. *He's* the one who's responsible for this mess." Arthur set the picture on the nearest table. "You need to help her with Nigel Farrington. You *must*. It's the very least that would be proper."

The old one brushed at her dress for a moment or two in thought. "Very well. Crystal… I shall make sure Nigel leaves you alone. Also, you are, ah, welcome to return for holidays and events. Perhaps once I adjust to this new information, I would consider more than that…"

Crystal blinked, stunned. "Y-you're not angry with me for what happened to Dana?" She choked up.

"No." Arthur came over and embraced her. "You no more caused what happened to her than you asked to be born."

"Would it be alright if I spoke with Mother?"

asked Crystal in a small, vulnerable voice.

Grandmother nodded once. "Yes. But… only if you tell her the truth of this. I am certain she suspects already. And who is this?"

"His name is Max Long. He's a private investigator helping me find out what happened to Dana."

"Ahh." The old woman changed the way she looked at me from 'bit of refuse' to 'acceptable servant.' She rang a small bell, which summoned Pierce.

The butler peered one eye around the door, as if afraid to walk into the room.

"Oh, knock that off," snapped Grandmother. "Crystal is not going to devour your soul. There has been a misunderstanding. She is no longer persona non grata. Please, see her to Sophia's study."

As if the man had never once given her a sour look, he smiled, then turned on his heel. "This way, madam."

Crystal glanced over at me with a 'you should follow me' stare.

So… I did.

Chapter Thirty
Reconciliation

Waiting in the room with Darth Grandmother didn't exactly appeal to me.

However, after an hour sitting on a nice chair near the sitting room where Crystal broke the news to her mother about the former Mayor Bradbury cheating on her... I almost wished I'd rolled the dice with the old one.

I didn't doubt Sophia Bradbury was Crystal's mother. By looks, they could've been sisters with a two-decade age gap. Crystal's more sylphlike, elven build came from her non-human father, and her mother had darker strawberry blonde hair. As soon as we walked in, I could tell the woman had long since fallen into a deep depression and probably spent whole days sitting alone and staring into space. The instant she saw Crystal, her mother brightened, clearly surprised at her being in the house. But also genuinely happy to see her.

So, I made myself as inconspicuous as possible, plopped down on a chair out in the hallway to give them some privacy, and tried not to feel too awkward as the resulting emotional storm raged on a short distance away from me. Sophia, unlike Gramzilla downstairs, appeared to possess genuine human emotions. Though, I will say that after the elder realized what a shit her son had been to Crystal, she did soften a little. Kinda lame the old woman only invited her back for holidays, but I suppose after spending the past eleven years thinking of her as a 'creature' with self-control issues, it would take her a while to adjust.

Still, that pissed me off. These people interacted with vampires relatively frequently and they thought *Crystal* was a dangerous fiend? The worst thing she'd ever do to someone is give a guy the best night of his life.

Anyway… over the next hour or two, Crystal danced around the subject of her not-father. It was as awkward and cringe-inducing as a Will Ferrell movie, but not at all funny. When she finally managed to get it out, her mother gasped, stared for a moment, then grabbed her in a fierce hug before bursting into tears. I'm no psychologist, though I've taken a bunch of online classes (learning how to read people comes in handy for a PI), I got the feeling anger at what her husband did to Crystal helped Sophia at least see over the top of the pit of grief she'd fallen into over his death. Maybe she'd even decided to be upset with him for cheating on her. Sophia spent a little while scolding Crystal for going along with the lie, but in the 'Oh my God, why would you ever do that?' sort of way, not actual yelling.

Sophia also appeared quite upset that Nigel Farrington wanted to abduct and kill Crystal, and utterly furious over the death of her older daughter. Though the woman seemed much nicer than the elder, I had a feeling relations with the Farringtons would soon become rather tense.

Our meeting with her mother elongated into staying for lunch. It unnerved me to watch the butler and some servants who'd initially reacted to Crystal as though some homeless drug addict had broken into the house were now all smiles and acting normal. I couldn't tell if they'd been artificially hostile to her out of fear of being dismissed, or if they faked the niceness now. It bothered me that I couldn't read them, though in all fairness, I'd only seen short glimpses of their nastiness beforehand.

I imagine whatever information network or gossip channel existed among the Founding Families had already started passing along word that Crystal had been restored to good graces with the family. That alone wouldn't stop Nigel, but it could potentially complicate things for him.

Eventually, we escaped. Or at least I escaped. Crystal didn't seem as relieved to get out of there as

I did. She also appeared to be daydreaming about finally being able to move back into the place. As soon as we returned to her car, I let out a long sigh of relief.

"Oh, they're not *that* bad." She glanced at the mirror and tweaked at her hair. "Except Grandmother. I still can't believe she actually listened to me."

"And I'm kinda surprised you forgave them so easily for how they treated you."

She gave me a 'what can ya do' look, then started the engine. "I'm too nice. But at least my mother won't have to sneak around to see me without anyone finding out."

"I can't even begin to comprehend how your father lied about you like that. Who *wants* anyone to believe they were seduced by their own daughter?"

"First of all, the man wasn't my father. Only on paper."

"Stepdaughter is still creepy as hell, even without the age difference. Is the rivalry with the Anworths really *that* bad?"

She drove to the gate and drummed her fingers on the wheel while waiting for it to open. "If I'd been a normal human, I don't think he would've gone there. Meaning, my being a succubus provided the perfect lie. As in... not his fault; not my fault. Truly, I have no idea how he would've handled it if I hadn't been such a perfect scapegoat. Brittany Anworth is also blonde and thin... the brief glimpse Mother got of her running off hadn't been enough for her to positively identify me enough to deny it when he claimed it had been me charming him. It was just assumed."

"Sorry."

"Not your fault, Max. The idea that Sterling Bradbury's daughter seduced him only sounds horrible to people who don't understand the truth. And really, no one outside the family even knows *why* I was sent to Ironside. Only that I was 'wild' or 'improper.' And, the people who were given the story about Mother catching me with him know what I am and believed I couldn't help myself. And he likewise."

The gate opened.

She drove out down the long, curving driveway surrounded on both sides by thick trees. It seemed somehow wrong to be driving a car here instead of a horse-drawn carriage.

"Again, no one outside the family knows the real reason I was sent to Ironside... except you. I realize the man's dead, but please keep that secret. About him and Brittany, I mean."

"Sure. The last thing I need is to piss off one of the Founding Families. Especially one related to the girl who's stolen my heart."

"Do you always talk like you're in a 1940s detective film?"

"They have specific classes on that at the private investigation academy."

Crystal laughed. "You are so full of it." She glanced sideways at me. "There's no academy, is there?"

"Nah." I smiled. "So you think this will work? With Nigel I mean. Can your grand—err, that woman really do anything?"

She shivered. "That woman has information that could end presidencies. She can keep Nigel away from me. It might only take her letting it leak to the other families that he plans to make an artifact like you mentioned."

"Sorry for butting in back there. I know you asked me to let you do the talking."

"It's all right. You made a good point and the look on her face when you inserted yourself into the conversation was priceless. Even if nothing else happened today, seeing that would've made the trip worth it."

"I take it the two of you won't be besties, then?"

She narrowed her eyes at me. "Do they teach understatement in the private detective school, too?"

"It's not a 'school,' it's an 'academy,'" I said with an overacted posh accent.

"Hah. And no. We never got along. I'm not Sterling's actual daughter, after all. Heck, the old bag barely tolerates Mother's presence. She once told me that she understood I didn't ask to exist, so she didn't blame me for that, though she felt I belonged at an orphanage and had been allowed to live there at the manor as a charity case."

"Ouch. Maybe she'll feel bad enough about the past eleven years to change her mind about you living there again?"

"I'm not sure, Max baby. Maybe. It did seem strange that she almost felt sorry for me. Maybe she's getting emotional in her old age." Crystal brought the car to a stop at the intersection between driveway and road, then turned left after a brief look in either direction. "The estate is all Bradbury. My mother is basically a guest. I'm sure if not for my two brothers, Grandmother would've sent her back to the Darceys. Since the boys are Sterling's offspring, Grandmother treats them wonderfully. I suspect she will eventually invite me back under pressure from Arthur. He is, after all, my half-brother, and as you could see, he seemed to come around and accept me."

"This is all like something out of medieval Europe."

"Basically." She jumped and eyed the rearview mirror. "Someone's coming up behind us."

I peered back at a newish Camaro full of high schoolers. "Just kids."

"Ugh. I'm going to be jumpy for a while. I hope they hurry up and do something with Nigel."

"What are you expecting them to do?"

She shrugged. "Like I said, it might only take her telling the other families what he wants to make. They'd all be petrified he'd turn it on them... and, in turn, silence him."

"Silence him, how?"

"The families have their ways."

"Do I want to know?"

"Hang around me long enough and you are bound to find out."

"Then I have every intention of finding out. Oh, and I would like to add, I have ways of silencing him, too."

"I know you do, and if it comes to that, we can discuss other ways to deal with that murderous asshole."

I admired the beautiful forest passing by around us, still not quite sure how to feel about everything that happened to me—or that vampires existed. I *did* know one thing... Nature gave me this power for a reason, and that reason appeared to be keeping the supernatural peace. I guess I'd become something of a sheriff myself, only for stuff no sane law officer would believe—or be equipped to deal with.

"So... what do we do from here?" I asked.

"I'm going to return to Ironside for a bit until things cool down. I don't expect Nigel to give up right away, but if I'm out of his reach, it'll allow time for the pressure to build and maybe get him to back off." She looked over at me. "Thank you for your help, Max."

Ouch. I involuntarily cringed at the client/PI tone of that. "Sure, happy to help."

"You will call me, won't you?" She batted her innocent blue eyes at me.

Whew. I smiled back at her. "Absolutely."

Chapter Thirty-One
A Stiff Drink

Two days later, I found myself again in my office, feet up on the desk, a tumbler glass of scotch in my hand.

Much to no one's surprise, I hadn't had any other clients show up. It's all nostalgic and romantic in movies when the PI can't get any work, but the reality of that absolutely sucks. Crystal did manage to talk her mother into pressuring the old woman, which resulted in them covering the repairs on my truck as well as sending me a modest bonus for making them aware of Nigel's apparent scheme to exert influence over the other families. The case might've turned my entire worldview on its head, but hey… my landlord got his rent and my truck was getting fixed.

The TV in the corner had been on for a while,

though I used it more for background noise, not really watching it. However, when the name Nigel Farrington went by, I looked over at it and started paying attention.

"… was found dead late this morning by three men headed out to fish on Bear Lake. According to Sheriff Justine Waters, Mr. Farrington had been in a disoriented state after being involved in an automobile accident on South Peak Road. Upon wandering into the nearby woods, he fell victim to an unspecified animal attack. Authorities are still investigating."

I swirled my scotch around, hyper-aware of what I must look like sitting here in my office. "Wow. I am a damn cliché after all." Chuckling, I held my left hand over the glass and summoned a pair of ice cubes, which fell into the glass with a soft *clink*. "Except for the magic, I suppose."

The TV moved on to other stories I had little interest in. I reached for the phone, intending to call Hank about the truck, see if it would be ready any time soon. But someone knocked on the door before I could find him in the contact list. Huh. How about that? A client.

"It's open."

They knocked again.

I set the phone and glass on the desk, got up, and cautiously approached the door.

Via the peephole, I observed a young twenty-something woman with straight black hair, leather jacket, spiked bracelets and dog collar, blue mini-skirt heavy on the 'mini.' Indigo-tinted stockings tinted her pale legs blue. Kind of a punk rock look to her. She shifted around, eyeing her surroundings like a teen who'd just shoplifted and thought someone noticed. Not getting any sense of threat from her, I opened the door.

"Can I help you?"

An air of staleness hung around the girl, like the never-touched bedroom in the house of an old person who lived alone.

"Hi. Are you a private investigator?"

"Unless someone randomly hung a sign accusing me of that on the wall outside, I guess I am."

"I'd like to hire you."

She didn't look like the type of girl who could afford to hire a PI. Hell, she didn't look like the type who could afford to eat at TGI Fridays, but then again, around here, looks were often deceiving. I'd been learning that the hard way.

I took a step back, waving my arm for her to come in.

She hesitated at the threshold, giving me a look like she tried to come up with something to say without being obvious about it.

Shit. I tensed like an Old West gunslinger about to throw down. "You're a vampire."

Her eyes flared wide for a second in an almost 'shh! Not so loud!' manner. "Relax," she said. "I'm here to hire you, not cause trouble. We're not *all* bad. If you don't need the money and don't trust me, just say so and you'll never see me again."

I studied her, face, body language, searching green eyes, smell... The staleness in the air reminded me of a crypt, but I couldn't say she *stank*. Not at all like Piper and Derek. They smelled like an unembalmed corpse left out in the sun. Hmm. Could that mean this girl wasn't as 'evil'? I'd been given elemental magic to create balance here. Balance probably didn't mean 'destroy all vampires.' Speaking of being a cliché, one of these days, a young, vulnerable-looking girl is going to be the death of me. I couldn't help but feel she had genuinely come here looking for help. Her nervousness made sense now, like a mouse seeking out the old tomcat to ask him something.

"All right. Fine. I'll hear you out. Please, come inside."

She relaxed ever so slightly and followed me across the room to sit at the client's chair in front of my desk.

I walked around my desk, picked up my scotch, and sat. "You'll forgive me if I don't offer you a drink."

The girl fake laughed.

I said, "Let me get this straight. You're a vampire, but you're not like the rest?"

She shook her head. "Most people would call me wild, rebellious, free-spirited... that sort of thing. I go my own way, but I don't take pleasure in hurting people. Whatever you've been told about us, we don't *have* to kill when we feed."

"But three bites… and you make more."

The girl nodded. "Yes, but there are ways to avoid that. Bloodletting into a cup for example, or donated blood, or even animals."

"So, what brings someone like you here to ask for help from someone like me?"

"My friend is missing. I'm really worried about him, and it's not something the police can help with."

"Okay. Who is this friend? What's she look like? Name?"

"He. Jackson Dolan. He's twenty-one, about your height, muscular, brown hair."

"Mm... hmm…" I jotted down notes.

"And he's a werewolf."

I damn near dropped the pad. With a sigh, I set down the pen, picked up my scotch, and downed it all in one swig.

I was gonna need a refill.

Stat.

The End

About J.R. Rain:

J.R. Rain is the international bestselling author of over seventy novels, including his popular Samantha Moon and Jim Knighthorse series. His books are published in five languages in twelve countries, and he has sold more than 3 million copies worldwide.

Please find him at: www.jrrain.com.

~~~

About Matthew S. Cox:

Originally from South Amboy NJ, **Matthew S. Cox** has been creating science fiction and fantasy worlds for most of his reasoning life. Since 1996, he has developed the "Divergent Fates" world, in which Division Zero, Virtual Immortality, The Awakened Series, The Harmony Paradox, and the Daughter of Mars series take place.

Matthew is an avid gamer, a recovered WoW addict, Gamemaster for two custom systems, and a fan of anime, British humour, and intellectual science fiction that questions the nature of reality, life, and what happens after it.

He is also fond of cats.

Please find him at: www.matthewcoxbooks.com